Advance Praise for The Deep Forest

"From this book spill hundreds of tiny seed-like tales, ready to burrow into the soft soil of your mind. They are strange, sweet, ruthless and profound, each hinting at briar-twisted paths to darker, wilder glades beyond your sight."

—Frances Hardinge

"A treasure chest of jeweled miniatures, all new fables and fairy tales from the fabulously rich imagination of Sofía Rhei."

—Lisa Tuttle

The Deep Forest

The Deep Forest

by Sofía Rhei

A Translation of *El bosque profundo*
by Kendal Simmons

Aqueduct Press
PO Box 95787
Seattle, Washington 98145-2787

www.aqueductpress.com

Library of Congress Control Number: 2025930061

ISBN: 978-1-61976-274-9

First Edition, First Printing, April 2025

Cover Illustration courtesy Anna Ribot Urbita

Book and cover design by Kathryn Wilham

Printed in the USA by Bookmobile

The tree opened, revealing its pages.

For Marian Womack and Rachel Pollack

Somewhere along the path of life,
in the belly of the Deep Forest,
to disorder the world decays,
when what was once good is now pain.
The path ahead tastes of escape,
that which is left behind deemed foul.
Nothing is certain, nor steady, nor complete,
and doubt raises a toast to desire.
The dark forest forces slow travel,
and to reflection Freedom is bound
when every memory, in a flood,
confuses its likeness, and it is the gift
lunacy, all love sickness,
there is no difference between Vice and Virtue.

Contents

Foreword

by José Carlos Somoza

Herein Lies Your Future

Shuffling

Dear Reader,

An extraordinary future awaits you. I will disclose a few things to you first. Not many. The future is yours to experience. Let us begin.

The Hermit

We tend to be one when we read. With this book, I foresee intense hours of peace and harmony. The solitude that is held in store for you is not abandonment: it is silence and a lamp, it is complete concentration, it is the company of invisible creatures.

The Mage

Ah, she had to make an appearance at some point. If you have not had the pleasure of knowing Sofía Rhei before, now is your moment. She has crossed your path, and she has power: soon you will not be able to put her books down. She is capable—and has proven so with this collection—of creating stories from the implausible, of playing with words before your eyes, of hypnotizing you with her plots. I know her well. I warn you of the influence she will have on you. A magical narrator, architect of fables, what Sofía does is no trick: it is a constant struggle to become better with each book that she writes. Here is her most difficult challenge yet, and she overcomes it.

The Lovers

Every book falls in love with its reader. The inverse does not always happen. But with this book, the love will be mutual, and at first sight. It is full of brilliant beauty and profound intelligence. How easy it is to fall in love! As Shakespeare once said of Cleopatra: age cannot wither her, nor custom stale her infinite variety. You will remain loyal to this book until the very last page.

Will you have children together? We shall see if Sofía ever writes a sequel.

The Stars

Dante concluded each one of his three Cantos with this word: "stars." He knew intuitively, perfectly, that literature was the best—the only—way to reach the stars. Sofía Rhei sows her space with tiny lights, tiny tales, with traces left by an all-powerful Tom Thumb in a black forest. You choose the path that you wish to take, but you will, dear reader, invariably trek further into the darkness.

The World

Each book is its own world. And those worlds are words. All words become a book. And each book is its own world.

The End

It does not exist: you will want to read it again and again.

The Deep Forest is extensive, but its paths are those that are etched in the palm of your hand. You choose where you will enter. It is said that only three paths exist, but where do they lead? Uncertain. It is possible to pass several times through the same place, and even more probable is that many of its corners will remain unknown. There are places that will always be found when searched for, and others to which it may take decades to return.

You will cross through thirteen doors, you will contemplate your reflection in thirteen mirrors, you will stop in front of thirteen trees, you will admire thirteen statues, you will find thirteen golden words, you will find thirteen ways to not answer a question. The forest demands things of you. It asks of you respect, reverence, fear. It reminds you of your fragile, animal existence, of the ephemerality of your fluid existence. The forest is full of exchanges, of pacts, of favors.

The forest does not have just one center. Its depths do not permit measurement, and even those who know the forest well all have different ideas of the number of steps it would take to travel its entirety. Everyone thinks that the center of the forest is its most important place, its most secret, but nobody agrees on where that is. The butterflies' clearing? The abandoned cabin? The fountain of those who suffer?

As you walk through the enchanted forest, be mindful of where you step. The harm or the good that is done to a single creature reverberates through all those of its kind, through different species, through those that feel the emotions of others, and even through creatures who do not share kinship with any other. You may prefer to avoid the wrath of the people of the Stinging Nettle.

Chapter 1: Paths

I

The Bellmaker

The Bellmaker never makes two bells quite the same. He gazes into the eyes of infants and entertains them in hopes that they laugh, though he also listens to their silences, which are not any less important. He designs rattles that turn the hasty patient and the lazy diligent. And, just a single glance will tell him all he needs to know about an individual. He knows which sound will cure them, and which will hurt them, and which will sadden them.

This artisan of bells lives in the River of the Turtles. He observes them, trying to make sense of the patterns on their shells, trying to make sense of the universe. Not once has he been able to make a bell for himself.

The Seer foretold a prophecy in which the princess would be made unhappiest by a man who possessed only one arm. So, the king ordered that the remaining arm of every one-armed man in the kingdom be cut off.

No one made the princess unhappy. But, scared of her father's brutality, no one took an interest in her either. Years passed, and she was offered neither affection nor company. The loneliness brought her to tears each night.

She asked the Healer for herbs so that she could sleep. That night, the princess dreamt that dozens of arms, all without bodies, invaded her father's bedroom.

The king woke the next morning, his skin full of scratches and bruises, all in patterns of five. They had torn one of his arms from his body. He then understood that the man destined to make his daughter unhappy was none other than himself.

JUST PAST THE towering rows of wild garlic, among fields of carmine flowers, and set right beside the Harp of the Rain, was a glass coffin. It contained the fragile body of the Girl of Thorns.

Her skin was a pale gray, her blue veins peeking through. With each breath, she would exhale an eloquent frost. Her thorns were of a darker gray, though almost black at their tips: a brilliant jet black, that of poison.

"Who will wake the Girl of Thorns?" sang the Harp whenever it rained. Her music was gentle with the passing of each summer shower, though thunderous when the clouds would storm. "Whoever wakes her shall die with the first touch, but only then will peace be brought to the forest."

The knights, soldiers, and travelers who heard the musings of the harp admired her beauty, but they did not wish to die. Among them, a boy had also discovered the glass coffin, all while searching for bellflowers to play with. The girl seemed very beautiful, but she also scared him.

Many years passed.

The boy, who was no longer a boy, returned each summer, and every summer, the girl filled his chest with fear. Be that as it may, he thought her even more beautiful, and he felt his compassion for her grow. One night, through relentless rain and charged with love, he could no longer resist the temptation to kiss her. He died in the act.

The Girl of Thorns awoke and mourned the death of her savior for three days, until he himself grew thorns. She placed him in the glass coffin and went forth to fulfill her destiny.

II

The Healer

"There is a snaking line of sick people who wait patiently to be attended by the Healer. At the same house, there stands another line, winding still, in which people also exercise their patience. Hidden in the shade are those who wait to see the Witch so that she might help them exact revenge on those who have hurt them. The Healer tends to her patients while the sun still shines in the sky; the Witch tends to hers beneath a frigid mantle of darkness and stars. No one seems concerned that they both live in the same house, that they both share the same face.

The Devil attempted to grow a tree, one with fruit in the shape of voluptuous bodies, so as to tempt men and women and draw them toward the warmth of his refuge (though some may call it Hell). He did not realize, however, that as his tree grew, so would another, one with celestial roots that reached down from the heavens and acted as a blight upon his realm, contaminating it with peace. Each attempt to remove those celestial branches only resulted in damage to his own tree. His branches, terrible and red, would shrivel to dust, to ashes, only to be whistled away by the slightest breeze.

After much thought, the Devil decided to stop hacking at this celestial tree, despite the undesired invasion upon his dwellings. If he wished for his mission to be successful, he should accept the presence of that steady spy.

When the men and women who devour the Devil's sensual fruit, who yield to loss and sin, reach Hell, they stop in front of that ashen, inverted tree and observe it, pensive, as if it reminds them of something, but they cannot quite make sense of its familiarity. The tree's merciful roots lick them and calm them, and from the tree flowers a fruit in the shape of their bodies, the bodies of the condemned.

WHEN A FAIRY drowns, which is a rather frequent occurrence, her spirit transforms into a round pebble and sinks to the bottom of the river. Only when another fairy, or perhaps a child, is able to recognize her among the rest of the pebbles and hold her in the palm of their hand will the pebble sprout wings and ascend to the sky, bestowing a wish upon the child or the fairy.

The little girl was so sad that she tripped and fell by the river. She felt as if she needed more than just her eyes to release all the tears she was holding back. She needed something more than what her body could give to express the immensity of her pain, the weight of it. All she wished for was to fade, to melt from sorrow and have the river's current carry her away.

When someone is that sad, it is difficult for them to recognize the fairies at the bottom of the river. And for that, her wish was not granted, and the girl lived.

And this is the truth about the pebbles in the river.

III

The Sensible Queen

She was so beautiful and virtuous that every time she spoke, from her mouth flowed blood-red roses. Those roses should not have been red, but only she knew their true color. Such wisdom had to be earned, however, as every rose has its thorns. And every thorn is sharp enough to slice.

The marks left by the wolf's claws were not disappearing, and her husband was set to return within a few days' time. She applied ointment in an attempt to hide from him the evidence of her infidelity. She loved her husband, but he could never give her the same passion, the same pain, that the wolf had aroused in her.

When her husband returned, his body was full of marks, like those made from a bird's beak. He said that he had been ambushed by the Master of Crows. She nodded and spoke not a word.

His wife knew the truth. She knew that this man-bird, so unsettling in his flocking form, had made love to her husband, destroying his skin, with an intensity that she herself could never match.

It is said that when a beautiful maiden dies before her time, the only way that her soul can reach its destination is by water. So, when misfortune strikes a family, prematurely robbing them of the most beautiful of their daughters, her funeral takes place by the river. Winter or summer, the children are sure to collect any visible flowers, keeping their petals from staining the untouched waters.

After night falls, at the river's hidden bend, she who gave birth to the maiden will examine its waters. If the water is white, she will breathe a sigh of relief. If the water is red, she will recite a prayer to the Earth. If the water is black, she will abandon the town forever.

SINCE SHE HAD never spoken a single word, everyone thought she was mute. She consumed only honey, which she ate with a golden spoon, one that was quite long and very small. She barely opened her lips, even to dine on such a fine treat.

There was a man who lusted after her, and he observed her for a long while. He planned his attack well, deciding he would kidnap her as she returned from the market. Since she could not scream for help, as she had never opened her mouth, never uttered even the gentlest sound, he would have every chance to do with her as he pleased. And there were so many things that he wished to do.

When he attacked the girl, her mouth gaped open in fear. The bees that lived inside her flew toward the assailant like irate arrows. They gouged out his eyes.

IV

THE TWO WARRIORS lifted their swords, ready to duel. One of them spoke but a single word, and with that he struck the fatal blow.

The Promise

"YOU MUST MAKE good on your word," said the prince after settling the kingdom's debts. "You promised to marry me."

"That was not what I promised," she said as she took out a sharpened knife.

She did not allow him time to react. She severed her own hand with a clean and experienced cut. She had practiced this many times before, in the kitchen. She bandaged the wound carefully as the prince watched, horrified by what she had just done.

"Here is what you were promised," she said, offering the prince her severed hand.

THE KING DID not trust his taster. So, he ordered the Mage to switch his eyes with those of a magical frog. He could now see even the smallest drop of poison.

The queen did not trust the king. So, she ordered the Mage to swap her eyes with those of a female wolf in heat. When she saw a red aura surrounding one of the courtesans, the queen knew that the woman genuinely desired her husband, not for his crown, but for his heart. The queen did not hesitate to have her killed.

The taster was in love with the queen. He spent years trying to poison the king, but, for some reason unbeknownst to him, the king had detected every piece of poisoned food.

The most beautiful of the palace cooks was in love with the taster. He never seemed to realize, though, because he was blinded by his own fascination with the queen. So, the most beautiful of the palace cooks gouged out her own eyes. She would never look at him again.

The Mage found the cook's eyes. Wanting to know the motive for which she had gouged them out, he placed them in a rabbit.

The rabbit went running to the taster. Frightened by its impetuousness, the taster killed the rabbit with a quick, fatal stab and brought it to the cook so that she could roast it. She put the rabbit in the oven without knowing that the animal bore her eyes and, as such, a piece of her very heart.

The queen tasted the smitten rabbit. She immediately burst into tears, washing away the wolf in her eyes. She finally saw the taster, who had never once shied his gaze.

The king could see that the meat was not poisoned. But, when he tasted it, his heart began to beat as it had not beat for a long time. It soon became too much. That echo of unrequited love reminded him of the rancor that colored his days. It sent him to the grave.

The Mage recovered the frog's eyes and gave them to the cook. She took a stroll in the woods and decided to stay there to live. What she saw in that forest was more than she had ever seen before.

V

The Memory

She opened the door that he had forbidden her from entering. Inside, a guardian owl suddenly appeared, as silent as the night. The owl devoured her right eye and ousted her from the room using his tremendous wings.

"Let that serve as a warning," he said as she returned home.

But she could not forget what her left eye had managed to see.

The recluse prayed to the Hollow Stone that the man she loved would love her in return. Each night, she dreamt of his embrace, she dreamt that he would caress her cheek, that a deep voice would whisper sweet, incoherent words into the curve of her neck.

The following day, the man searched for her to tell her that he loved her. However, it seemed that a terrible accident had disfigured his face the night before, and the woman realized that her love for him had been nothing more than a caprice.

She decided then that she would instead love another man, the man who had always loved her. The next day, however, she tripped while holding scissors in her hand, and her face was left with a terrible gash. Her suitor fled, frightened by her disfigured appearance.

The recluse then prayed to the Hollow Stone that she would love herself. The following day, when she saw her wounded face in the mirror, she understood that a visible scar is much better than one inside. She knew that, eventually, she could be content with what she had.

SHE BELIEVED THAT all jewels were simply chains and shackles, representations of punishment, of possession. Necklaces were yokes, bracelets were shackles, and rings enslaved in the worst of ways. That is why she preferred to adorn herself with poppy and honeysuckle during the summer, with hellebore and crocus in the winter.

She gathered so many flowers that it drew the attention of the Herb King. He decided to punish her by taking away her beauty, thinking she would no longer feel the need for such ornamentation. Blood did not flow through the king's veins, but rather a phlegmatic sap incapable of producing fear, and so he did not understand why a woman would do such a thing if she did not believe herself to be beautiful. He did not understand that she was ashamed of her ugliness, of the wrinkles that would soon form.

Panicked by her rapidly aging face, she gathered more violets, more of the lovely leaves of red ivy, more of the tiny white flowers that grew between the rocks that paved the spring. She desiccated them and spread them over her body. She even ate some. The more flowers she picked, however, the more her skin withered and dried, the more her eyes sunk, the more her lips cracked.

The king finally realized that she could not hear the soft laments of the flowers as she uprooted them and was thus ignorant of the pain she caused. So, he decided to turn her into a plant, bestowing upon her the ability to hear the steady pulses of the earth. It was then that the bellflower was born.

When they are withered and aged, their pale green petals turned to gold, bellflowers will ring softly with each gentle brush of wind, as if to say that they have finally accepted the warm beauty of their years.

VI

He Who Collects the Morning Dew

He is interested in all types of droplets: the tears of someone in love, the drops of rain that fall during an unexpected shower, the spit of a babbling baby, the drool of someone fast sleep.

No one knows for certain why he collects these drops. What could he want with them? To whom does he sell them? Impressed by his elegant attire and enticed by the splendid prices he pays, very few individuals refuse to sell him the droplets he seeks.

He is occasionally seen pouring the droplets he collects into the river, pigmenting it ever so slightly. No one dares to ask what will happen to those who live downstream when they drink the tainted waters.

A dead serpent can never rest. When a serpent dies, she is condemned to an eternal search. She must find the shed skin of another snake, and there she must live until the skin is old and torn.

One of these serpents could not find any such skin, and so she sought refuge elsewhere, eventually finding an empty reed in which to live.

A young musician cut the reed to make himself a flute, without realizing that in that reed lived the ghost of a serpent. The flute sang such beautiful melodies, melodies that captivated all who listened, permeating their memories until it was there that they remained. And, oh, how they hurt.

WHEN HE WAS born, the boy had a mark on his fourth finger, like the mark left by a ring. The witch knew what this mark meant. She explained to the boy's parents that the Ghost Queen had chosen him to be her husband.

The boy's mother tried to erase the mark using any means she could, but it was impossible. The boy's father then decided to sever his finger entirely. It was useless, however, as the mark reappeared the following day on the other hand. His mother cried and cried, begging her husband not to sever that finger, too. She knew that the mark would never disappear.

By his eleventh birthday, the boy had grown to be so beautiful and kind. Everyone had come to care for him. Every one of them feared the day that the capricious queen would call upon his presence, and he would never be seen again.

However, the queen never came. To the relief of his relatives and acquaintances, the boy did not disappear. He became a dashing young man, despite never marrying, and the townsfolk eventually forgot about the legend. Even as he aged, he maintained a youthful glow, which most people ascribed to the nutritious berries he ate.

His mother, however, knew the truth. She knew that her son, forever young, would outlive them all, even the grandchildren of the grandchildren of his siblings. She could not imagine a fate more sorrowful than that.

VII

The Wise Woman and Her Books

There is a woman, loaded with books, who drags her cart from town to town. Each time she comes across a storyteller, a song-singer, or a playwright, she writes down their stories. The task may take her weeks to complete, sometimes even months. It is impossible to know when she might return to each town with new books to lend or old books to collect.

Some folks are so happy to see her that they gift her with bells. Others, when they hear she has arrived, cry, hugging their books tightly, refusing to let them go.

It was written that one of the nine sisters had to sacrifice herself to the dragon so that the others could live. The littlest sister, who had always been the bravest, read all that was written about dragons and offered to go. She promised that if she were to survive, she would find a way to communicate it to the rest of her sisters.

"Did you know that dragons are born when a flaming serpent incubates a brown chicken egg?" said the girl to the dragon.

"How ridiculous," replied the dragon, showing her, painfully, exactly how the children of dragons are made.

A year had passed when a mouse arrived at the house of the other eight sisters, carrying in its mouth a cord tied with three knots. They understood that their sister was pregnant with the dragon's child, and so they went to speak with the witch. She explained to them that the dragon would devour their sister the moment that she gave birth to that horrible creature. The sisters asked the witch for a magical remedy, and so she gave them an acorn. As long as their sister kept this acorn, she would remain pregnant without giving birth. The mouse carried the acorn to the littlest sister.

Nine years passed. The dragon's wife continued to communicate with her sisters until one day she told them that she was tired of living with the dragon and that she would prefer to give birth to her monstrous child and be done with it once and for all. And so, she threw the acorn into the river and immediately went into labor.

The dragon nervously awaited the birth of his offspring, but in place of a whelp with scaly skin and yellow eyes, from the womb of the woman a child was born. After having spent nine years in the body of a human, the dragon had nearly turned into a boy.

"This is what happens when a chicken incubates the egg of a serpent," protested the dragon, disgusted.

Scared by that prodigy and believing that his wife was a great witch, the dragon freed them both. The woman and the mouse reunited with the other eight sisters, and between them all raised the boy with yellow eyes.

VIII

The Girl and Her Scale

There is only one way to know if a love letter truly comes from the heart. There is a girl who travels from town to town with a scale made of clinging reeds, and one must await her arrival if they wish to know the truth. She will weigh the amount of sincerity that each letter contains and the intensity of the writer's affection for their beloved.

Liars feign concern as they wait for the girl's arrival, while those who speak the truth are afraid that their passion does not burn brightly enough.

There was a monk who cultivated peas, and he found one that was perfectly golden. Taken aback by this miracle, he was unsure if he should plant it, eat it, or offer it as tribute to his goddess. He decided to sleep on it. That night he had three prophetic dreams, and each one indicated a different path.

The monk deliberated for three weeks until he finally came to a decision. He dug a bed in the dirt, ate the pea, and prepared himself as an offering to his goddess. From his tomb sprouted the most incredible stalk that had ever been seen. It nourished all who were in need, and its tallest tendrils seems to touch the sky.

THE FRUIT OF the orleta are shaped like small cages or miniature prisons. The gorzes started using them as prison cells to hold captive the wives of their enemies, the punzes, since the punze females produce a milk similar to the milk of the incredibly savage gorzes. Time is precious when at war with the punzes, and it makes little sense to waste it on the tedious tasks that survival demands.

But the gorzes only see the milk produced, not the tears that are shed. Trapped in their cages, they cry into the orleta. With time, the plant comes to understand their message.

Inside each cage, a sharpened spear is beginning to sprout, and its blade looks oddly similar to the ear of a gorze.

IX

The Perplexed Man

The hermit admired the splendid suit of the emperor, but he failed to understand why people laughed at him and said that the emperor was actually naked.

The crabs that live in the White River of Deep Forest are incredibly evasive. To catch them is nearly impossible thanks to their astuteness. But, if they are captured, they writhe and twist about themselves and even go as far as to consume parts of their own body. The fishermen think that such a habit makes the meat of these crabs especially nutritious, and so the meat is fed to children with the hope that they grow up to be strong and healthy. Those living along the bank of the White River rarely live to be less than ninety years old. No one suspects that if they were to stop eating these crabs, those ninety years would turn into two hundred.

Eszter noticed that the hole in the trunk of the willow was the exact size of her finger, and so she decided to stick her finger in. Upon its removal, she saw that her finger now wore a wooden ring.

"The tree has gifted you one year of its life," an old man told her.

Eszter, content that she had an entire year for herself, thought about the best ways to spend it, and she decided to write a long poem to the willow tree. That afternoon, however, she was invited to the town dance. She thought to write the poem later.

At the party, she met a boy with eyes so intensely green they almost scared her. They barely talked, but by the end of the night, they were kissing in the shadows, and the boy's kisses tasted of zephyr.

They saw each other every day that year, and Eszter found not one day to write. She did nothing but think about the mysterious stranger, despite never even knowing his name.

After some months passed, the boy disappeared without a trace. Eszter was too sad to write the poem she had promised the willow.

When a year had finally passed, she returned to the spot where she was given the ring and saw the old man once again.

"I've wasted the year," she said crying. "I had hoped to write a poem for the willow, to forever sing praises of its wisdom and beauty, but alas, I have done nothing but enjoy myself...and here I am, with my heart broken."

"You have not wasted a single day," said the old man. "You wrote the poem with your kisses and with your joy."

It was then that the old man transformed into the young man with green eyes, and Eszter realized that before her stood the spirit of the tree, and that the ring that she wore on her finger was not only a gift, but a question, too.

"I do," she said, her face glowing.

The tree smiled. His shrewdness had been worthwhile: in exchange for just one year, he had received an entire lifetime.

X

The Bars

It was said that his lute had magical powers, and that it could control the minds of those who listened to its music. Because of this, the governor ordered his arrest.

He used the bars that lined his cell as a musical instrument, and the beautiful sounds convinced the people of his innocence.

There once was a mother so hungry that her breasts no longer produced milk. She plucked one leaf from the sacred tree and was arrested for it.

The priestess, an opulent young woman with brilliant hair, grabbed the leaf from her hand and shoved it into her own mouth. The priestess's tongue immediately shriveled and dried, and she aged nine years. The soldiers, scared, released the mother.

As the poor woman returned home, her breasts filled with juice.

"Mama, you taste like fruit," said her little one.

Death does not communicate through stones, but rather flowers.

The tombs that lie below fertile land allow us to see the truth about the souls who rest there, thanks to the flowers that grow in the spring. If any doubts exist about the innocence or guilt of an individual, the presence of true rose or of bloodreed serves as evidence. If they kept secrets, dive lilacs appear; if they were happy, wave lily. These flowers have no actual bearing on the fate of the dead—instead, they show those who still have their senses the best way to use them.

THE TREASURE HUNTER carried with him a small army of woodpeckers, tethered to him with string, to help him search hollow tree trunks. A very large and very wise black pig also accompanied him during his travels, and he was able to dig up even the most impressive trees, the favorites of the misers.

One day, an old lady asked him for spare change, and the treasure hunter refused. So, the old lady turned his woodpeckers into goldfinches and his great black pig into an adorable, meowing kitten.

The treasure hunter had no choice but to change professions. He would make a living going from town to town, sharing the sad stories he read in the many unrequited love letters he found while looting. The misers received these letters and would bury them along with their money.

It was then that he met a woman who pitied his sensitivity and offered him her heart. But the treasure hunter was not a true cantor. At his core, he was still a treasure hunter, which is quite like a miser. He was not capable of responding in kind.

So, the woman cursed him. She turned his goldfinches into bats and his kitten into a lone wolf, condemning him to live only by night.

The treasure hunter remembered when he had first become a treasure hunter: that night, so long ago, when he had witnessed an old miser bury a box. Bats swarmed around the miser, and a wolf howled in the distance. Upon closer inspection, there were no gold coins in that box, but rather a love letter. So many years later, the treasure hunter still wondered how a letter could be considered more valuable than riches and gold.

XI

He Who Makes the Signs

The Signmaker traverses the forest, walking each path as they are indicated on the signs. He does this to see if the signs remain true, or at least, to see how such a sign could be justified. He has gotten lost so many times that he now no longer knows what it means to be found. He emends, corrects, repaints, adjusts, and annotates.

The Deep Forest is riddled with signs nailed to tree trunks, signals nailed to posts, wooden arrows, milestones, landmarks. They are written in the most variable of languages. Sometimes they only show a simple symbol, open to interpretation. Not all the signs are exact, let alone comprehensible. Some have been diverted by the wind or by birds, while others refer to places that no longer exist. Many of them used to be traps, and they very well could still be. However, it is not the Signmaker's job to warn others about the signs of the forest, as naive as they might be.

It took the luthier three years to build that violin, following the exact instructions of the queen. She had asked him to use the blackwillow wood and a varnish made of bitter cedar, veleaf, and boraz. The luthier knew that these were plants used by witches, but he kept the secret, his mouth sealed shut by the gold doubloon he received each week.

He delivered the piece. The following day, there was a terrible storm, and the king died. The entire kingdom mourned his loss, as he was a very kind king. Feeling guilty, the artisan sat below an almond tree and saw a musician just as sorrowful as he.

"I wrote a song that killed the king," confessed the musician, his gaze down. "His son requested that I write it with the singular blue feather of a goose. Like the ones used by mages, you know?"

The luthier told his story, and both men debated for a while over which of them was more responsible for this regicide. As punishment, they decided to write a song lamenting their sins, after which they would take their own lives.

Thirteen months later, they reunited in the same place. They sang the song, took their own lives, and unleashed a terrible storm that once again saved the kingdom's crops, just as it had done the year before. The god of rain was cruel, only to be satisfied with the most painful of human sacrifices.

At the palace, the queen and the prince cried for both musicians, just as they had cried for the king.

THERE IS A legend that reads: "the tree that has caterpillars in place of roots will devour your hands, but in exchange, it will grant you wisdom." If this legend did not exist, a great number of charlatans would not feel obligated to amputate their own hand, just so that someone would listen to them.

XII

The Ruby Flower

As the ruby flower was uprooted, he heard her cry out in pain from the depths of the shaking earth. He quickly regretted his greedy decision and tried everything possible to bury the flower once again, to return her to her original state. Before he could, her roots enveloped his hands and dragged him toward the earth. Though much too late, he realized why rubies are so vibrantly red.

The Lightwings' ship sailed the Lavender Sea, floating gently on the mist of its pleasant aroma. Only insects could see this mist, and so they would move out of the way, often as a sign of respect.

On one particularly translucent summer night, there was a little girl who could see the ship's reflection on the surface of the water. She then began to worry that she herself had somehow turned into an insect. She carefully observed her body, fearing with certainty that terrible changes were to come. That fear, that anxiety, was what drove her to take her life.

Even in death, the little girl, who was perhaps an insect, continued dreaming of that boat as it floated through the air. Inside the tomb, her dreams crystallized into an iridescent rheum, a rheum the color of lavender.

As the queen woke, they told her that she had not given birth to a baby but rather to a hairy monster with terrible fangs. Everyone expected the queen to be horrified, to reject the child, but she instead asked that they bring him to her. She offered him her breast, just as she would have with any other baby, white and beautiful. The whispers soon began. The king trusted in his wise and gentle spouse, and so he made any vilification of her character a severely punishable offence. The king trusted his wife, and yet he still did not understand how she continued to care for, and even love, a being so different from herself, so different from the king.

One fine day, the queen called upon a miracle-worker. The old woman walked slowly toward the palace. Her hair was braided with shells, and she wore a very long necklace made of flowers that reached her feet. Everyone agreed that if anyone could create miracles, it was she. Shortly after her arrival, the baby transformed into a normal boy. The king paid the miracle-worker generously and ordered everyone to attend mass. He filled the cathedral with flowers and ordered that the bells be rung in celebration the entire day. He did not tell anyone what he discovered in his wife's room: a small pair of scissors and an even smaller file. They were next to a large pair of scissors and an even larger file, worn from use.

XIII

The Wild Boar

After having killed the young boar, the hunter found an intact nut in its mouth: the tusks of the beast did not cause even the slightest scratch. He tried to pry open the nut using all his force but could not. He carried the dead boar home and gave the nut to his daughter for her to play with.

The little girl, without speaking a word, placed the soul of the beast between its tusks once again. It rose from where it had lain and ran away.

They found her mute, covered in a viscous fluid similar to the albumen of an egg. She stared up at the sky, as if she were waiting for something that would never come. She refused to move until the storm drenched and defeated her.

Years passed. She created a round nest out of sticks, straw, and feathers, and she kept it scrupulously clean. Her family put bars across her windows. She never remembered how to speak.

He considered putting a bell on the Muse so he could track her movements. He would then know when she was near, and when she was not, and could save his energy by only working in her presence. No bell existed that could be placed around the neck of an incorporeal being, and so he asked a ghost to make one for him.

The ghost smiled and accepted the commission, only so long as the poet would write him a poem about his life.

"But if the poem is not good," warned the ghost, "I will take you with me."

The poet accepted, confident in his ability to succeed. When he had the intangible bell, he waited for the Muse to appear. With a false caress, he then hooked the bell in her hair. Once hooked, the bell was no longer visible, but its jingle could still be heard.

He made good use of the Muse's presence that day to write a beautiful poem, after which he fell asleep. He left, went to the tavern, and wasted not one moment writing if he could not hear the subtle ringing of her bell. Sometimes days would pass without a sound. Other times, months.

When he finally gave the poem to the ghost, the ghost replied with anger, saying the poem was horrible.

"That's impossible," said the poet. "It's the only poem in the world that has been written completely under the guise of the Muse."

Then, with a smile, the ghost removed the bell from his hair. The poet protested, saying that he'd been tricked. The ghost burst into laughter. As he dragged the poet to his frosted and frozen realm, he said:

"Who are you to call yourself a poet, and yet do not know to distinguish between the Muse and a ghost?"

"THE WOLVES ARE not the guilty ones. Guilty is the demon that possesses them. You see, they are especially vulnerable creatures because of the great solitude in which they live," said the hermit, his maw still wet with blood.

XIV

The Cook

THAT MAGIC CLOTH, with a texture so like the smooth skin of a young girl, was the only thing that could heal the maladies of the old cook. But the moment the princess laid her eyes on that cloth, she decided selfishly that it would be hers to keep. She said that she would not change out of the dress she was wearing, not until she had one made from that magic cloth.

The old cook died as soon as the princess slipped into her new dress. It was then that the garment clung to her body and fused itself to her, wrinkling her skin like that of an older woman.

She had been a princess but soon realized that she could now only be a cook. She asked where the kitchens were, made her way toward them, and began to prepare vegetables for a broth.

THE DOOR WAS marked with some sort of symbol, either a flame or a claw. The mother, who was always careful to watch for possible threats, noticed the symbol and tried to erase it, but it was impossible. That night, she left pillows in her children's beds and took them to spend the night elsewhere.

The elves came to the marked house, but they did not find the chosen children. In their place had been sacks of feathers and cloth. So they granted their powers to the pillows instead.

Days later, the woman decided to return home. The mark on the door had disappeared. In the years that followed, the pillows taught the children all the elvish songs and legends while they slept. Without realizing it, the children learned their language.

When they announced to their mother that they were leaving home, she was furious and demanded an explanation. The children confessed that the pillows had been speaking to them for years now. The mother stabbed the pillows with a kitchen knife, and though they bled, she could not stop herself.

When she turned around, she saw that her children had lost their eyes and ears.

She smiled, relieved. She would finally know peace. Her little ones would never leave her side.

"THE WHITE PIPS of the pomegranate belong to the fairies," her mother used to say. They should not be eaten. They should be set aside with care, spread on a blue plate, and placed by the back door. By the time the night falls, they will have disappeared.

"And how is it that the dogs don't eat them?"

"The dogs also know that the pips of the pomegranate belong to the fairies."

Despite her mother's warning, the girl thought that no harm would be done if she were to eat just one.

The girl vomited later that night, and in the sanguine puddle there was a small, minute larva. Its wings had already begun to sprout.

XV

The Pumpkin

They cracked opened the pumpkin, still hot and steaming, and found inside a roasted suckling pig. Inside the pig, there was a turkey, and inside the turkey, a rabbit, and inside the rabbit, a perfectly boiled goose egg. In place of its yolk, there was a red apple, raw and gleaming.

The woman, a newlywed, doubted for a moment. Ever since she was a child, they had warned her about apples. She did not dare slice further.

Her husband, so as not to exasperate the banquet's invitees, guided her arm, and together they cut the apple.

A black serpent slithered out of the fruit, so quickly that all they saw was a black streak. The bride thought she heard a hiss, or the slightest hint of a hiss, that murmured:

"Thanksssss."

A peasant, a priest, and the devil, who possessed the beautiful body of a woman, were arguing over the immortality of the soul.

"Only those who follow a righteous and holy path will live forever," said the priest, his gaze fixed on the devil's body.

"I believe that all beings are good-natured, one way or another. It matters naught if we live forever," said the peasant.

"The word of God is clear on the matter," warned the priest.

The peasant thought for a moment.

"Tell me, Father," he asked. "Have you ever died? Because I do not talk about that which I do not know."

The devil burst into laughter. The priest and the peasant did not know at whom she laughed. The devil then spat on the floor, and from her spit grew a stalk that, once mature, sprouted yellow bean pods.

"This is my favorite plant," she said, her voice lovely and tender. "Only those in possession of the truth can touch it without burning themselves."

The priest snorted, taking a step back to distance himself from the plant. Suspicious, he said:

"Who is going to fall for your tricks and traps? How could anything that comes from your mouth be worthy of my trust?"

But the peasant approached the plant, examining its stalks and leaves, and tore off one of its pods.

"What are you going to do with those seeds?" asked the priest, alarmed.

But the peasant did not answer. The next day he took off on a long journey without telling anyone where he was going. He never returned to his village.

Sometimes, these strange plants, with pods as yellow as sulfur and fruit as red as ember, can be seen growing by the entrances of many churches—the priests, however, always have burns on their hands.

TRADITION STATES THAT the youngest witch will pass down her name and face to the next generation through a ceremony in which she submerges her head in a river.

The face of the budding witch is then carried by the river's current to the village where she was born, and, from the water, she says goodbye to her loved ones.

The village's youngest girl is then brought to bathe in the river.

XVI

The Monster

When the girl grew older and no longer had those terrible nightmares, the monster found a way to escape. He then stole a body and asked for her hand in marriage.

She did not recognize him.

Like so many times before, the boy went to show his mother the cricket he found. This time, however, it was not a cricket.

"Why do you look so scared, Mama?"

His mother smiled and placed the devil in a cage, just as she would have done with a cricket. The devil flapped his wings in response, and all the crystal and porcelain in the house shattered to pieces. His mother realized, too late, that she never should have caged the devil.

"You don't like being trapped, do you?" said the boy.

He then took the devil from his cage, gave him a kiss, and released him back into the world.

"I learned my lesson, Mama. I'll never again cage another animal."

But his mother heard not a word. She could only watch as her son's lips turned yellow. Yellow like sulfur and sickness.

SHE PROMISED HIM her hand in marriage if, in return, he promised to never look at her after midnight.

After some months had passed, her husband, in a wine-induced stupor, forgot his promise. He opened the door to her chambers and searched for her in every corner. He could not find her. He did see a painting, however, that he had never seen before, hanging there on the wall.

He approached the painting and observed it. It was a still drawing of fruit, opulent and fleshy. It was depicted with astounding realism. There were two grapes, a small winter pear, a strawberry, two red apples, two peaches, a watermelon…

Eager, the husband stretched his hand toward the grapes. Inebriated as he was, one of the grapes seemed to materialize before his eyes, and so he ate it. He then fell asleep.

The following morning, his wife was missing an eye. In its place, there was nothing but fair skin extending smoothly from her forehead down.

XVII

The Mandrake

A Mandrake child is born twice: first from the womb of its mother, and then once more, after its petite body is buried in the dirt, its head above ground. Its eyes, green and bright, stay shut for days, only to open when buds begin to sprout.

She never told anybody that the baby she carried in her womb had been conceived by a human, but everyone realized the truth when the child she planted never sprouted.

When the woman was with her husband, she always wore impeccably elegant clothes. He never saw her with even the slightest hair out of place.

That is, until he followed her to the house of her lover. For the first time, he saw his wife in ragged, worn garments, like the kind that peasants wore. He discovered the true color of her lips, which he had always seen covered in a carmine gloss. It was then that he realized his wife had never truly loved him.

She had been given the cruelest of curses: to be so beautiful that men would try to force themselves upon her. Even her own brother, whom she trusted to protect her, tried to seduce her one night. Sick of living in fear, she decided to escape. She traveled hidden beneath a cloak made of wolf's fur, so frightening that it could scare anyone. She avoided people and tensed every time she saw a man in the distance. She preferred to walk along the city walls and fields of thistle.

One day, after many months of travel over moors and down weathered roads, she heard a voice through a gap in a wall—and it was indeed talking to her.

"Please, help me!" she heard.

The voice was terrifying, but she stopped.

"I've fallen victim to a spell. A mage turned me into a boar. I can't leave my garden because I am too scary, and naturally, no one is permitted to enter."

"That doesn't sound too bad," said the girl, still dressed as a beast.

"I can only return to my human form if someone looks at me without fear."

She thought about it for a moment. She had been alone for so long.

"I am not afraid."

"You're the first person who has stopped to talk to me. Do you wish to help? I will give my eternal love to whomever frees me."

"I'm not afraid of wild boars, so I believe I could look at you without fear. But I *am* afraid of men, such that your eternal love will be of no use to me."

The man-turned-boar was intrigued by the sound of her voice and thought that it was perhaps better to be loved in such circumstances than to not be loved at all.

"I will love you even if you don't turn me human."

She climbed the wall and saw his splendid garden, free of men. She covered her eyes with a cloth and leaped into the beast's territory.

"You are my equal," said the boar.

She nodded. She thought that, after all, the boar used to be a man, and she believed that if she were to see his true form, he would attack her just as all the others had done.

They lived happily together. He would bring her fruit and she would gently pet his fur. She would sing to him, and for the first time, she felt protected. No man would enter the garden of a true beast.

One night, she realized that she was grateful to the boar. She thought about how he had always wished to be a man and decided to gift him her fearless gaze so that he might finally be happy. When she removed the cloth that blinded her, she saw that it was not a beast by her side, but a man.

"You tricked me," she said.

"Yes. I am so beautiful that women only desire me because of my appearance. I invented the tale of the beast so that I could find a woman with a heart as pure as yours. And I did."

She understood that, of all men, he would know to respect her beauty, and so she finally removed the fur that cloaked her.

"I don't care what you look like," she said to him.

He hugged her. It had been quite complicated, but he had finally managed to seduce the most beautiful woman of them all.

XVIII

THE BOY WAS certain that the expression "new moon" meant that every month the old moon would wither and fall to the ground, leaving behind a replacement. And so, he spent the nights before each new moon walking through the forest in search of the old one. He thought that she might be very cold and sad, and so he wanted to comfort her.

One night, he finally found her. The sky was dark, illuminated only by the stars, but on the surface of the lake shone a radiant full moon. She had fallen in. The boy waded into the freezing waters and swam until he reached her warm reflection, a faithful rendition of her true brilliance. He then held her in his arms, and together they ascended high above the lake.

ON THE COLDEST day of winter, an ice flower will sprout near the edge of the lake. As dawn welcomes the morning sun, the plant is nothing but a fragile stem. It then grows branches, sharpened by the cold, that soon burst open with petals. By the time the sun sets on the horizon, those flowers transform into perfect spheres. They conserve their chill, never melting, even after years.

During the coldest weeks, certain animals are occasionally seen walking through the forest. They seem almost transparent, as if carved from ice. They were never taught not to eat the ice flower's frozen berries.

Do not touch the ice flower with bare hands. You'll feel the heat leave your body, and you'll fall ill for weeks. Some say that is all that happens, but others warn of a cold even more dangerous, one that reaches the depths of your very heart.

The Keeper of Secrets

THE PRINCESS COMPLETELY ignored anything that made her sad, and because of that she was incapable of understanding the people of her kingdom. The elderly king asked the embroiderer to make the princess a coat that expresses the pain of his subjects, even the pain they keep most hidden. Each day, a new subject would come to the embroiderer's tower, and she would pluck a single hair from their head. She would then thread the hair through a needle while the person in question would whisper to her something unthinkable, translating it into the language of symbols and thread, tracing silent figures with her art. But the embroiderer warned the king that simply knowing the hardships of others is not the same as having lived through them.

When the princess put on the coat for the first time, she drew back in surprise, and the first white hairs appeared on her head. The subjects distanced themselves from her, ashamed that she could feel their sins and secrets. But it was then that the princess thought that she could perhaps become queen. She felt prepared. The king died peacefully, certain that he was leaving the kingdom in good hands. The princess, now queen, named the embroiderer as her royal advisor.

One good day, a woman went to ask a favor of the queen, who was imparting justice in her cloak of pain. The woman's husband had stolen her children from her, claiming that she had been a bad wife. He claimed that those children had been conceived through an act of infidelity and belonged to another man. But he needed them to work his fields.

The queen considered the situation and ruled in favor of the husband. The mother had not respected the rules of matrimony and as such, had lost her rights. The embroiderer, without speaking a word, took the cloak from the queen and draped it around the peasant woman. She began to sob uncontrollably as she felt the abrasive weight of the cloak resting on her shoulders.

The queen finally understood that it was not the same to know the pain of others as it was to live it, to experience it. She returned the children to their mother, named the embroiderer ruler of the kingdom, and left to discover the world for herself.

XIX

The Old Woman and Her Bees

The bee woman carries a hive above her head. Some of the spongy golden insects respect her. Others hate her, which is why she is always covered in stings. She can't hear anything because those tiny creatures have built walls of wax inside her ears. But when the bees leave, as they sometimes do when they go looking for flowers, all the children flock to the bee woman to drink the honey that drips from her fingers.

At the cave's entrance, he found a bird frozen in a stalactite, though it had been partially melted by the sun. It was the most beautiful, most sorrowful thing that he had ever seen. The immobilized bird seemed as if she were about to sing.

To prevent the ice from melting any further, he carried the bird deeper into the cave where the sun did not shine, where there was only shade and darkness. The cave's echo multiplied the marvelous song of a bird by a thousand and one times. Strangely though, there were no wings, no flapping, to be heard.

The dryad made herself a dress using autumn leaves, and when she put it on, she won back nine years of her life. The girl, who watched the dryad from where she hid between the thick trunks of the forest trees, made one for her aging mother. Maybe the dress would work for her, too.

However, after putting on the dress, her mother became much younger than anticipated, even younger than her own daughter. She was also much prettier. The boys that had previously given their attention to the girl were now blinded by her mother, though they did not recognize her for who she was. And so, the mother forgot about her daughter, all because of her recuperated youth.

The girl then returned to the forest and made a robe from tiny white flowers. Her skin wrinkled instantly, her hair turning the color of snow, and the dryads accepted her as one of their own.

XX

The Iron Chain

"The day on which that chain breaks, you will lose your sanity," said the witch to the king.

It seemed to be a good deal to the king. It was a very sturdy chain that would undoubtedly outlive him.

He ordered the witch to be killed. There and then, one of the links turned to wax.

The fairy hunter does not catch many fairies, but he hunts with determination. Every day, he puts on a new disguise so that those shrewd little creatures, with their unbearable giggles, don't recognize him and devour him on sight.

Or, well, so he thinks. The truth is that the fairy hunter dies every day, devoured by the fairies. His memory is transferred to another body, even more ridiculous than the last, so that the fairies can keep laughing at him.

The magic cradle belonged to the entire kingdom. When a child was born, his parents would bring him to the cradle so that he might sleep for a few hours, and any ailment that the boy had experienced hitherto would disappear.

After the queen gave birth to her daughter, she decided that the cradle should be exclusively for the princess and should therefore remain at the palace. When the queen placed her daughter in the cradle, all the illnesses from the other children loomed about her. The king came in time to grab her from the cradle and save her life. Her mother returned the cradle to the town hall, but it had already lost its powers. They left it in a storage room and soon the whole world forgot its existence.

The princess survived but was always sick. She was ugly and deformed. The mere fact that she was to be observed by others was torturous. The residents of the kingdom made cruel jokes at her expense, and bets on how difficult it would be to marry her increased with the passing of each day.

One day, however, a beautiful young man appeared and asked for her hand in marriage.

The princess talked with him for some time and got the impression that he was kind. So, they married.

Within a year, they had a daughter. She was quite possibly the ugliest baby imaginable. Even the paintings on the walls dared not to look at her.

It was then that the princess's husband asked her to come with him to the town square. In front of the crowd gathered there, the handsome young man held his daughter in his arms, and at that moment, his body transformed into the magic cradle. The daughter of the princess instantly turned beautiful, and so did the princess. The townsfolk cheered and decided to make her queen in place of her father.

She did not accept. She let the cradle stay at the town hall and declared that all the children of the kingdom could sleep in it, but she never left its side.

XXI

The Empty Cave

Every few years, townsfolk would forget why that cave was named Dragon's Mouth, and every time they did, someone would eventually wander in. Its jaws would then close shut, devouring them whole.

Such is the wisdom of the animal.

The bird flew to the top of the tower and, through an open window, looked into the Mirror of Wisdom. It was now so much more than a bird. When it saw the lost hero in the Forest of Forgetfulness, the bird guided him to the highest floor of the tower and showed him the mirror, the one that the hero had forgotten he was searching for.

When the hero saw himself reflected in the mirror and recovered his memory, he remembered that his objective was to do away with every abomination in that enchanted kingdom.

He turned to the bird with the intention of killing him, but as he did, he caught its gaze. He and the bird were now equals. The green eyes of the hero and the black eyes of the bird turned to quicksilver, and they could no longer see.

They now guard the mirror, one on each side, forever.

The king's crown was adorned with twelve silver eyes. When he wore it, he could see what was happening in each of the kingdom's twelve provinces, and he could speak with their leaders, who also saw him. One day, he fell asleep. His daughter, who had never left the palace, could not resist the temptation to put it on.

The next day, the twelve sons of the twelve leaders arrived to ask for the princess's hand in marriage. She said that she would marry he who could take her farthest without ever leaving the palace.

The first told her stories of his many travels, but she was not immersed in the stories he told. The second showed her a mirror from lands far away, so that she could see how it might be in another country, but she only saw herself. The third showed her a telescope, but there were only images on the other side. The fourth sang her a song from the other side of the world, but the princess did not understand its language. The fifth took her to the top of the palace's tallest tower and told her about each of the twelve roads that parted from its base, but he could not answer all the princess's questions. The sixth dressed her in strange clothes and explained the customs of other women, but it was not enough. The seventh danced with her. The eighth gifted her various perfumes. The ninth showed her paintings. The tenth cooked for her. The eleventh gifted her with costly maps. She said that nothing was good enough.

Then, the twelfth spoke: "It was I, dressed as a servant, who put a soporific in your father's drink so that you could wear the crown and others would come to show you the world." And the princess married him.

XXII

Memory Fog

It was not a ghost. It was the fog, though it took the shape of the girl whom he still loved, even ten years after her death.

The ghost, as always, was a figment of his imagination.

And the fog was simply fog.

Written above the threshold was an inscription:

"This is the Door of Poetry. Whoever crosses it shall understand its mysteries."

But nobody dared cross it. Some were fearful of understanding the mysteries behind the door, and others, of understanding their own. It was rumored that Simon, the town lunatic, had entered through the door twenty years ago. It was now impossible to understand the strange words that he spoke.

That's what Gala thought when she observed the door, wondering if she should enter. She thought it might be the only way to keep her parents from marrying her to an unbearable man. Any sane person would hate whoever passed through that door, and so she that's what she did.

When she returned, her beauty had completely withered away. But Simon looked at her as if he had never seen someone so lovely. He talked with her, and Gala understood perfectly each and every word that he spoke.

PROVINCIAL LAW STATED that only reciprocated love could be true, such that everyone who declared their affection but did not have it reciprocated were accused of falsity and thrown in prison for two years. If after those two years they continued to feel their unnatural feelings, and the object of their affection still did not love them in return, the individual would remain incarcerated for double the amount of time, in succession.

The oldest prisoner was eighty-six years old. And he was still in love with the woman who created that law.

Chapter 2: Fountains

I

Ace of Fountains

What the Waters Take

There are many springs sourced from subterranean waters, though it is best to be cautious around them.

The waters drag, they make disappear, they snatch. They also clean, of course, but they tend to clean that which we hold most dear. Water can take many forms, but the spring is the most deceitful of them all.

The most treacherous waters are those that cause thirst.

It is not quite true that the Siliken drive travelers mad; that they gift them with the ability to hear everything so precisely; that they make the traveler aware, without warning, of just how chaotic, disorienting, and deafening their own thoughts can be. It is also not true that they achieve this by morphing their faces into the face of whomever is standing in front of them, just to show them all that they could have been—a truly monstrous imitation. It is true, however, that the pupils of their eyes are the color of mercury, reflecting whatever image lies before them. The reason that travelers lose their minds is not because they see their own image, cruelly and fearfully deformed, reflected in the Siliken's eyes, but because their eyes, rounded and argent, reflect the inconceivable vastness of the universe.

When she abandoned him, he made a cut deep in his arm and promised himself that he would forget her by the time the wound healed.

But the wound never healed. Instead, silver fish began swimming through his veins.

He thought they might be caused by the pain as it tried to leave his body, and so he opened the wound up a bit more so that the fish might be freed, so that the pain would finally subside. As the fish passed from his arm and into the river, they dissolved like tears.

The last silver fish abandoned his body, and the wound healed.

He felt a chill echo through his chest. He realized, a bit too late, that the fish were not born of pain. Rather, they were remnants of his very soul.

THE GIRL OF Thorns journeyed through the forest until she reached a castle. It belonged to the Girl of Dreams. She hid behind the hedge to observe how the washers washed the clothes, how the embroiderers embroidered, how the gardeners gardened, and how, in the kitchen, the cooks cooked partridge.

It was then that the hedge opened, revealing a path that invited her into the garden. She reached the center without anyone noticing, except the Girl of Dreams.

She observed the Girl of Thorns and nodded her head. She then climbed the 444 stairs that spiraled up the tallest tower. She took a single breath and then pricked her finger on the jet-black spindle of the spinning wheel.

As she fell to the floor, the Girl of Thorns sunk her feet into the earth, and from the tips of her toes sprouted roots. Her hands and legs transformed into thick, spiny stems. They grew and grew until they surrounded the entire palace.

The washers stopped washing, the embroiderers left their embroideries unfinished, the water flowing from the gardeners' watering cans halted in its path, and even the partridges, which were being grilled on skewers, stayed perfectly still.

II

Two of Fountains

The Dragonflies

"It was the dragonflies," said the girl as the crops burned. "Don't you see them?"

There is a nursery rhyme that white witches sing, and some say that it turns normal girls into witches. That is why mothers will cover their daughters' ears when the white witches pass through the town at night, singing their song.

There is something that those mothers do not know: the song is not what turns little girls into witches. It is the desire to hear it. When their mothers cover their ears, the little girls destined to be white witches feel a burning curiosity, an ardent desire, as they imagine what the forbidden song might sound like. They soon escape from their houses, running straight to the forest, begging one of the witches to sing her song.

There are many more locks in the world than one might think. They are all around—it is only a matter of noticing them. All the keys that have fallen into a river, carried away by its current, only to be confused later with the shine of a fish's scales; all the keys that were forgotten in the hollow of a tree trunk or beneath a doormat; the ones abandoned in gutters; the ones stolen by animals; the ones that slid through the hole in a bag only to fall on the green moss covering the forest floor. All the keys taken by the sea so that she might turn them to rust, to coral; the ones stolen by magpies; the hundreds of thousands of keys sold in flea markets. All those keys belong to a lock somewhere in the world, locks on doors, windows, wardrobes, dressers, drawers, chests, trunks, and arks. Locks that sit there waiting, locks whose histories echo against the emptiness of their interiors, and locks who open their mouths to sing their histories aloud.

Keymaster can hear the song of their pasts. He is invisible by virtue of his plain attire. He dresses just as anyone else might dress, and he never looks a person in the eyes. He does not walk too fast or too slow; he knows the right streets and the least traveled sidewalks. He smells ever so slightly of copper and brass. He smells like a place that has stayed closed for far too long. When it rains, he disappears completely beneath his enormous black umbrella, which he moves slowly, never disturbing anyone.

Sometimes, he stops for a second, hesitates, and then changes direction, almost as if he forgot something somewhere. Or, sometimes, he simply continues on his way but takes each step with a bit more purpose. When a soft jingling is heard, somewhat reminiscent of the sound that glasses make during a toast, you know he has found a new lock.

III

Three of Fountains

The Three Cats

"If you don't go to sleep, the three cats will come to find you," said the boy's grandfather.

The boy stayed very still in his bed, thinking about those three cats and their eyes that glowed red like the seeds of a pomegranate.

Time passed, and he himself had a grandson. He remembered how terrified he was of those three cats, and despite knowing that they would come seeking his grandson, he refused to instill in him that same terror.

That night, the old man could not sleep. And despite the fact that he would never rest well again, he smiled, because he knew that he had protected the person he loved most.

The salt tasted different, like sulfur. The fisherman then realized that beneath the waves, the sea harbored a hell of its very own, and he pitied the sirens.

The lake was so vast that shells could be found in the depths of its waters, and some of them even had pearls. Kids would dive down deep, as far as they could, hoping to grab just one of those shells. Gifting a blue pearl to a loved one was said to have guaranteed their heart forever. Many died in the attempt.

There was a girl, not yet sixteen years old, who continued to dive again and again, though she was already exhausted. On her last attempt, she returned to the surface, shell in hand. With bated breath, she opened the shell. Inside, she found the largest and most perfect blue pearl that had ever been seen.

When she returned to the town, she looked at the window of the house of the man she loved and decided to knock on his door.

"I've got one. How much will you give me for it?"

His eyes brightened. He needed the pearl to win the heart of the town's most beautiful maiden. And the fifteen-year-old girl needed the money so that her family could keep their house.

She spent the night in tears.

Her beloved spent the night observing the pearl, rolling it between his fingers, until the morning sun rose above the horizon, catching him by surprise. Suddenly, things were no longer so clear.

IF HE CARESSED the wind for long enough, in the right way, the sleeping girl would always appear. He would then watch her for as long as he pleased. He was very careful not to wake her, though, for she would disappear the moment she opened her eyes, becoming wind once again.

IV

Four of Fountains

THEY BURIED HER after she died, failing to heed her warning: that she was a woman of the Mandrakes. You know how whimsical some spinsters can be! Nine nights passed, and her nine children popped out of the earth. They devoured the heads of all the townsfolk.

That is why, in every town within the confines of the Deep Forest, it is essential that someone be able to translate the language of the Mandrakes. And, of course, the language of the spinsters.

The Hedgehog and the Rose

THEY COULD BE observed from a distance. They were different, yet the same. Neither of them made any effort to hide the fascination that they felt toward one another. They admired each other, feared each other. And each day they grew more agitated, more impatient.

One morning, they found the rose destroyed, its petals torn to pieces. They found the hedgehog with a great thorn piercing his heart. Their wish, however, had come true. That very night, a rose without thorns and a hedgehog without quills were born.

THERE WAS A flower that could cure any sickness, but it only grew when the wisest of the dryads was on her the deathbed.

The prince, desperate to find medicine for his mother, poisoned the wisest of the dryads and stayed at her side until a flower sprouted from her navel.

With her last breaths, the dryad lifted her arm, slowly plucked a single petal from the flower, and placed the petal in the prince's mouth. The prince was cured of his wicked intentions, and with tears streaming down his face, he gave the dryad what little remained of the flower.

The dryad took those remains and parted them into two pieces of equal size. She then parted those two pieces into four, and then sixteen. Each piece was the same size as that very first petal. The dryad made as many petals as there were people in the kingdom, and only after she finished, could she finally rest.

THE PRINCE ARRIVED at the castle, his quicksilver sword in hand. He hacked through the vines and thorns that surrounded it, unaware that with each cruel strike, he was killing the Girl of Thorns. The prince woke the Girl of Dreams with a kiss, and the entire castle came back to life. She mourned the Girl of Thorns for three days. Then, she married the prince. The Girl of Dreams said that she could never kiss him, and he accepted the condition. They were happy for four years.

One day, however, it was the Girl of Dreams who forgot, or decided to forget, her curse. She kissed her husband, who immediately began to grow tired. With a sigh, she helped him lie down in the same spot where she had lain for years, waiting. Then, she left.

V

Five of Fountains

In that town, it was said that nothing healed an old person's sores better than scabs from the scalp of a nursing infant. It is unsurprising, then, that they sold for such a good price at the market.

Brilliance and Happiness

The smiling princess's teeth were so bright that when they disappeared, the entire kingdom grew sad. There was one little boy, however, who thought that he might find her teeth in the magpie's nest, and so he did.

The boy realized that the magpie was in fact the Spirit of Sorrow, and he knew that she was important, as joy cannot be felt without the presence of sorrow. He waited for the magpie and asked that she exchange the princess's teeth for his own.

The magpie accepted, since the boy's smile was even brighter than that of the princess. When the princess finally faced the public once again, dressed in her finest clothes, the crowd rushed to see her and trampled, unknowingly, a small, toothless beggar.

The magpie, which perhaps was not just a magpie, devoured her new teeth. Nothing nourishes sorrow as well as the voluntary loss of happiness.

The princess's dress had 999 buttons. None of them had any purpose, except one. Unbuttoning that single button was enough to undo the entire dress.

The princess's suitor knew that if he could figure out which button would undo the dress, he would win the heart of the princess, cunning as she was, as well as the blessing of her father, a well-known philanderer. Since the suitor knew that he would only have one chance to figure out which button would undo the dress that night, he decided to consult two expert dressmakers. He managed to sneak them into the princess's chamber as maids. One of them, the less famous of the two, looked at the suitor as if she were in love with him.

That afternoon, each dressmaker told him that a different button would undo the dress. And when the suitor was finally standing in front of the princess, she said:

"I've never told any of my previous suitors which button is which, but you're different."

And she pointed to one of the 999 buttons on her dress. It was not the button that the dressmaker who was perhaps in love with him described, nor was it the button that the other dressmaker pointed out.

Her suitor thought for a moment. If he chose the button that the princess showed him, and it worked, it would mean that the princess chose him out of all her other suitors, despite barely knowing him, and that did not make much sense. If she showed him the wrong button, that would mean that the princess had no interest in him, which was something that the suitor had no interest in discovering.

If the button that the enamored dressmaker had shown him was the correct one, then that could mean she prioritized his well-being over her personal happiness—or it could mean that she was simply not in love with him. If she showed him the incorrect button, then she would have the chance to marry him, instead of the princess. But he did not want a lying, egotistical wife, regardless of how well she could sew.

The suitor unbuttoned the button indicated to him by the other dressmaker, the more expert of the two. The dress fell to the floor in a cascade of silky gauze.

He then realized that nobody loved him. He left the room, then the castle, and then the kingdom, in search of a new princess.

VI

Six of Fountains

The Old Lizard King

He does nothing else besides lay in the sun, and he rarely smiles. Disturbingly so. Occasionally, his quick hand, which is deceptively wrinkled, closes its fist around the reptiles that frequent the wall.

They say that he only eats lizard tails. That is how he managed to live such an astonishingly long life. In town, they speak of him with respect, with a certain admiration.

Very few know that he also eats lizard tongue, not just their tails. That way, he can whisper his own words through the mouth of any one of those elusive creatures, wherever they might be hiding.

Lizards can weave their way in and out of any nook, which is why so many walls whisper incomprehensible words, fragmented and frightening.

The old Lizard King kindly greets the same children who are terrified of his many voices, his many tongues. That is the part he enjoys the most.

Throwing pebbles at a girl's window with the intention of seducing her never works. But, if instead you throw exactly nine seeds of wulfspirit, in intervals of equal length, the girl will have no choice but to open her window and listen to what you have to say. You know just how expensive those seeds are…and their impact against the glass almost always breaks them.

But, of course, this is just the beginning. It is not enough for her to open the window. You also must capture her attention. You can do this by rubbing a bit of powder on your forehead—not just any powder, no, but powder made from the larvae of a simar. Its fresh scent will awaken her curiosity, although it will reek for three days after as the powder ferments.

Neither the seeds nor the powder will do anything if you fail to say something interesting, so don't forget to wash your tongue with white rennet, which stimulates loquacity—though you'd better be able to tolerate strong spices.

With this advice, it should be easy to win over any girl you wish. That, however, raises a new issue: Which will you choose? You will know which girl is right for you when you do not have any of the three ingredients, and, yet these three simple tricks still work.

THE GIRL WAS absolutely certain that she would grow wings if she ate the proper foods. Because of that, she ate only the gray, bitter wings of insects and gnawed tirelessly on all those foul-smelling bird feathers.

VII

Seven of Fountains

Twin Wells

The Well of Hope returns the will to live to those who have lost it.

Across from it sits the Well of Despair, which lowers the expectations of those who have too many.

It is impossible to drink from one but not the other. The key is to drink from them in the right order.

Goodvine only wraps itself around those who are destined to have children. Some couples are brave enough to approach this plant after their wedding night, to sit on the rock by its side and wait.

She begged him not to make her do it, but her new spouse was adamant and impetuous. He wanted to see if the legends were true. They both fell asleep. When they woke in the morning, they saw that the vine had not wrapped its tendrils around them. He was furious, and in his fury, he destroyed the goodvine. He tore it out of the ground and stomped on its roots.

"If I can't have children, then neither will you," he swore to the plant.

However, months later, his wife became pregnant. He laughed, knowing that the legends about goodvine were nothing more than superstition.

"Why did you destroy it, then?" she asked her husband, her voice filled with sadness. She no longer loved him.

In her womb, she would not find a baby, warm and round. No, it had spirals, thorns, velli. It rubbed its leaves, coarse and rugged, against her flesh, fighting to escape.

After her husband suspected her of infidelity, the young mother was abandoned in the forest. Freezing, and unable to feed her son, she needed to find shelter. She followed a mother bear, discovered her cave, and confronted the terrible animal so that she could stay in the den. She struck the bear on the side of her head with a large, heavy rock and drove a stake into the bear's flesh. The two children, the newborn bear and the baby boy, sobbed, terrified of the violence.

The woman was incapable of killing the cub, and so she raised him alongside her own son. Both learned to walk and act like men. The cub learned to speak, but the more he talked, the less fur he had. His face changed, softened, over the years, until it looked like his brother's.

It was then that the woman's husband returned to find his son, as a failed second marriage had left him without an heir. The abandoned mother observed him for a long while. She then showed him both children and asked him to identify his son.

Without hesitation, the husband chose the bear and took him with him. The little bear resisted, and it took several men to restrain him. That, however, to the ignoble father, was just more proof that the young male was his progeny.

When the bear realized that they were trying to take him away from the only mother that he had ever known, he forgot every word that he had ever learned and transformed back into a bear. He killed all the men and brought his mother enough meat to last the entire winter.

VIII

Eight of Fountains

He wanted to construct a pair of wings so that he could fly further than any other human. But, as he worked, the Singer of Truths passed under his balcony, singing this tune:

"That which lives and breathes shall grow and fly,

That which dies and decays in the earth shall lie."

Somber, the boy who had so wished to fly stared down at his work. The table was covered in feathers plucked from rooks, starlings, and crows, from owls and falcons. He breathed in their pungent odor, heavy and cruel.

He furrowed his brows. Perhaps these wings would not allow him to soar, but they could certainly take him further than any other person had gone before.

The Teaspoon Maker

He used to be a knife maker. He would imagine the curves, the angles, of each knife; he would fantasize about each gesture, each movement, that would land the blade between someone's ribs. His daggers cost five times more than the average knife, as only his knives could provide such a silent death. He always said the same thing when making a sale: "This metal is forged in water, as made obvious by its shine."

He came to regret all the violence he brought upon the world and decided to leave the business of knives for that of teaspoons. Children and the elderly eat soup with spoons, and that can only be good.

The maker of teaspoons never passed through the same town twice. Perhaps, if he had, he would have realized that his teaspoons, as thin as blades, often found their way into his customers' hearts, or lodged in their stomachs. The knife maker's teaspoons were also forged in water.

AFTER EVERYONE ELSE had left, though he was exhausted after a long day of work, the monk whose job it was to draw illuminated initials decided to stay a bit longer. He let his finger rest on the manuscript and watched as creatures began to rise from the illuminations where they hid during the day. They crawled from the pages, onto his finger and then up his body, licking his skin and his eyes as they did.

IX

Nine of Fountains

The Mother Bear Dead in the Snow

The hunter saw a dead bear in the snow and recognized her as the animal that he had tried so many times to hunt and kill. Each one of the scars that covered the wise beast told a story of persecution and rage. The hunter, in reverence, removed the bear's liver, a symbol of her bravery, and fed it to his three sons, hoping that they might absorb her strength and poise.

That very night, the hunter noticed that the bodies of his three sons were covered in wounds. The hunter knew, as he had seen many wounds before, that they would never heal.

The prince made it clear—the only way to free her beloved from the gallows would be to spend the night with him. She had no choice but to accept, and so she did with gritted teeth. She could not help but cry the entire night. The prince admired her integrity and sacrifice.

The following day, exhausted, she was reunited with her husband. He was furious and said that he would rather be dead than so shamefully dishonored. He said that he would have no choice but to kill her, that the life of a wife was worth less than the honor of a husband.

When the prince discovered she had been murdered, he went to find her husband, and they fought each other to the death.

In the Other World, the prince found the woman and declared his love for her, saying that he gave his life to defend her honor. She said, in response, that she could love a murderer, but not a man who failed to keep his word.

Her husband then found her and declared his love, saying that he had given his life for her cause. But all she said was that his death was worth less, so much less, than her honor.

SHE WAS TORMENTED quite frequently by the same nightmare: each strand of her hair transformed into a long, slim, writhing worm that fought to detach itself from her head. Those that managed to do so would flail about in search of her mouth in an attempt to slither in.

She always thought that this dream meant her own thoughts were trying to poison her, and so she decided that she would no longer have any. She would distract herself with many tasks. She would embroider, cook, organize her spices. But the more she tried to control her thoughts, the more frequently she had that nightmare. It was exhausting. One night, she decided to cut off her hair, hoping to never have that nightmare again. She missed one hair, however.

That very night, in her dream, the very last of the white worms managed to crawl into her mouth. When it did, she felt an overwhelming sense of peace and gratitude, as if this nightmare would never return. This warmth flooded her mind and welcomed her spirit.

X

Boy of Fountains

ALONG HIS FLESH, he drew the image of a keyhole

Perhaps there existed a key that could open his chest and extract the pain that had been consuming him for so many years.

If such a key did not exist, he would have to find another body on which to draw it.

THE NEWBORN SPRING

ITS WATERS SING a cheerful melody. They laugh and bubble as if an infant, not even a few months old, were splashing about.

However, nobody plays in its waters anymore.

The ghost of the little drowned girl tries to tell the others with her sweet laughter that they should not be afraid, that the view from the water is so much better than the view on land. It is almost, *almost* as good as never even having been born.

WHEN HIS BELOVED died, the prince ordered that a harp be made from her hair. The music that flowed from that instrument was marvelous and pure, but it was impossible to strum any song that was not tremendously sorrowful.

The prince discovered that in every song, regardless of which minstrel or troubadour played, the word "apple" would appear.

He thought it might have been a message from his dearly departed wife, and so he spent all his time in the apple orchard. He observed the leaves as they sprouted and watched the flowers as they budded, until he saw the fruit that they bore. When it came time to harvest, he was surprised by the beauty of one of the farmers. Her eyes were sad, her hair the same color as the hair of his beloved.

It was then that he understood. He went to the artisan that had created the harp, who then confessed that he had not used his beloved's hair.

"Her hair was not fit for music," explained the artisan, fearful of the prince's reaction. "Her hair could not produce even the slightest sound."

The prince forgave the artisan. He realized that the miracle worked by his late wife was simply different from what he had imagined.

The Magic Window

The princess was not exactly beautiful, but she possessed a magical window that made beautiful whatever was seen through its glass. She always sat by the window, and the knights who caught a glimpse of her would never fail to ask for her hand in marriage. Of course, her greatest pleasure, as the ugliest of all the princesses, was to reject each and every one of them.

XI

Maid of Fountains

Despite the fact that the blue berries were healthy and curative, no one ate them because one out of every seventy was so spicy that your mouth would continue to burn for days. Everyone ate the delicious white berries, however, which sweetened even the sourest of memories, even though one in every seven hundred was deathly poisonous. It was said, as it is always said when something is terribly true, that it is nothing more than a legend.

The Compassionate Fish

There exists a fish that can launch itself out of the river and into a fishing net, but only when he who holds the net is truly starving. That day, however, the person who turned to the river for help did not need sustenance. Rather, she yearned for love. The fish jumped into her lap and told her, as it breathed its last breath, that she was to cook it and feed it to the man she loved the most. Before the fish died, the young woman gave it a kiss on the lips.

She did as the fish had told her to do, and she stewed it with green onion and wine. The man devoured the meal so quickly that he was barely able to enjoy it. As soon as he had taken his first bite, however, he stopped for a moment to look at the young woman, as if he were truly seeing her for the first time.

When they kissed, his lips felt aquatic and slimy—it was strangely reminiscent of that very compassionate fish.

THE MONSTROUS WOMAN stared at herself in the mirror, with just a candle to light the room. She could only stand to look at her body bit by bit, piece by piece: her nose, too long; her eyebrows, too bushy, too asymmetrical; her lips, overgrown and simply horrendous. She was certain that she could not handle seeing all her ugliness at once. Those who *had* seen her, however, thought she was quite beautiful. They could not help but admire the harmony between her strange features, features that on any other face would feel out of place.

XII

Jack of Fountains

The Pearl in the Glass

As she handed him the pearl, the witch said:

"Whoever she loves, and loves truly, will turn invisible to her."

The jealous husband dissolved the tiny, gray pearl in his wife's drink. It would take nothing more than a sip for her to forget her lover forever.

After dinner, he offered his wife the glass. She closed her eyes as she drank. She then smiled, thinking her husband was playing some sort of game, and asked him:

"Oh, now just where have you gone?"

He discovered that if he spoke the truth, his breath would smell horrendous. But, if he lied, his breath would smell of fresh lime and jasmine. The smell of his breath was more important to him than the truth.

Yielding to the fisherman's pleas, the siren finally gave him her magical net. All that he would need to do is toss it on top of any woman to make her love him forever.

"Choose wisely," warned the siren.

But the fisherman, who knew patience was his greatest weapon, was only pretending to be the siren's friend. He had been in love with her for years now.

He threw the net over her, and she cried out in anguish.

Many years later, she died. Neither of them was ever happy.

The fisherman could not help but open her corpse, just to see what she looked like on the inside.

Just as he had suspected, her siren heart was full of spines.

It had not been her fault.

WHEN SHE WOKE from one of her dreams, floating around her, although just for a moment, were iridescent fragments like the wings of a dragonfly.

She knew that if she was awake, it meant that the insects who carried her soul to the Land of Dreams had died. She cried inconsolably, but that did not bring them back to life, their wings shattered by the light of day.

XIII

Sage of Fountains

A LUMBERJACK SWUNG his hatchet as he tried to cut down the tree in front of him, but a white flower blocked his path. Instead of slicing the flower in two, the hatchet broke.

He understood, in that moment, that the tiny plant was home to the spirit of the most powerful warrior, and so the lumberjack wanted to take that strength and make it his own. He tried to pick the flower apart with his hands, but they just bled. He tried to bite the flower, but his teeth shattered instead. As he was about to give up, his hands bloody and his body hurting, he tried one last thing—he breathed in the scent of the flower.

When he did, he forgot his name, and the spirit of the most powerful warrior possessed the body of the lumberjack.

The Guardian of the Well

THE GUARDIAN OF the water in the well asks three questions to every person who arrives, anxious to possess the coin that could make their dreams come true. Only if the person answers these three questions quickly will the guardian know that their wishes are indeed authentic. At the first sign of doubt, the coin will turn to dust in the wind, and so will its guardian.

THE YOUNG WOMAN noticed a man with braided hair laughing in the tavern across the way. Next to him was another woman, her hair white with age. The young girl could not understand how a strong, handsome man like him could prefer the company of a woman as old as she, so thin, and with a nose so crooked. The young woman was the most beautiful woman from the neighboring village, and she thought that it would be a simple task to attract the attention of the man with the braided hair.

She knew that he was a lumberjack. She followed behind him as he ventured into the forest and quickened her pace until she was ahead of him. She stepped on one of the hunter's traps in hopes that the lumberjack would find her and free her.

That he did. He cured her wounds and gave her a kiss. She then held on to his braid as he carried her back to his house.

The following day, the young woman's mouth was full of pustules. The lumberjack knocked on her door, but she refused to let him in, thinking about the terrible rumors that would spread about the woman with white hair, saying that she was a bitter and vengeful witch. The young woman decided that she would never see or speak to the man again.

The man with the braid, worried about the young woman, had returned to bring her the antidote to the poison with which the hunter laced his traps.

XIV

Elder of Fountains

The Bird and the Old Man

It is said that the rook can live three lifetimes. In the first, he simply observes. In the second, he is gifted with the ability to understand spoken word. In the third, he gains the power to grant one wish, though always the same.

The old man whispered his last words before the rook, and his granddaughter became pregnant.

With his increasing age, the man barely slept. That is why the kingdom he built in his dreams was falling apart, slowly, piece by piece. He had no time to fix the buildings, or to care for the forests, or to wind the clock in the tower.

He always assumed that this kingdom belonged solely to him, that it was a figment of his imagination, but one day he heard a knock. He opened the door only to see an emissary, one that he recognized immediately, considering that he himself named him at birth. Aldor was his name, and he told the man that the kingdom did indeed exist and that it was located on the other side of the world.

"I have only come to tell you that we recently discovered that you are the man responsible for the existence of our kingdom, for its upkeep and its betterment. For some time now, each and every one of us, each and every night, have tried our best to dream that you, Sir, will live forever.

The assassin threw the body of the handsome young man into the river, staining its waters with blood. The fish drank so much that they learned to speak his language, and they came to understand his heart. They swam until they found a beautiful young woman, and they told her of what had happened. She cried and cried until the river was once again salty, and the fish drank her tears. Their scales hardened, their eyes darkened, and they grew teeth.

The assassin was sleeping soundly on the bank of the river.

Chapter 3: Doors

I

Ace of Doors

To him, the eyes of the crow were the most beautiful eyes he had ever seen, and he wanted them for himself. He thought that with eyes as beautiful as those, women would simply fall at his feet. The next day, he woke with the eyes of a crow and ran screaming from his hunting partners.

The Door Where Mystery Beats

As you stroll through the Deep Forest, you may come across doors with no building attached to them, arches that have no infrastructure to support. It may seem as if these doors lead to nowhere in particular, but it is best to avoid them. It is advisable that you stick to your path, especially if the doors are open, almost as if they were inviting you inside. To force one of their locks would be the equivalent of trying to hurt yourself with your own teeth.

The writhing root scared all those who passed by, which is why the seeder of seeds pulled it from the ground and threw it into the river—she hoped that the current would carry the plant far from there, to the sea, and that the salt water would put the root to rest.

Unbeknownst to her, there is nothing more energizing to a writhing creature than water in motion. The writhing root prospered. It grew and grew until it occupied the entire riverbed.

The seeder of seeds realized her mistake and asked he who guided the water to guide it back to the river, which had now run dry. She knew that this would delay the coming of the spring, and that it would cost her years of her own life. There are some mistakes that turn into winters.

FOR THE SAKE of all mankind, the inquisitor was determined to find exactly where in the body the soul was kept. So, he experimented with those sentenced to death. He severed their limbs, sliced through their skin, and extracted their viscera. He then tested each body part against the Feather-Bell test, just to see if each still bore the weight of the prisoner's soul.

His experiments were of no use. All the prisoners, even those who committed the most horrendous crimes, and whose most intimate and spiritual parts were extracted from their bodies, seemed to have kept their soul.

One night, the inquisitor dreamed that he himself was measured against the Feather-Bell test. The next morning, he drowned himself in the river.

II

Two of Doors

The People of the Arches

They live beneath bridges and can adopt any shape or form. They ask for a toll, for your nostalgia, your rancor, for the love that beats so gently, so softly, inside your chest. That love in your chest, your heart, it beats differently when you catch a glimpse of that person you thought was dead, or simply lost. Those beats provide the nutrients on which they survive.

Beneath the fair maiden's balcony waited a long line of suitors. Each one sang of their virtues. Each one described how they kiss differently, better, than the last.

She had never kissed anyone before, though she learned from books and stories that there existed only six types of truly magical kisses. There was, of course, the kiss that awakens, and the kiss that puts to sleep. The kiss that poisons, and the kiss that cures. The kiss that gives, and the kiss that takes. Given that she was neither sick nor somnolent, and since she was neither dying nor did she wish to be, she did not care to hear about her suitors' kisses. Too many risks for such a small reward.

But then came the minstrel, who sang about kisses that quenched thirst, that tasted of fresh raspberries, that rang like the chimes of a small bell. It piqued the maiden's curiosity.

She kissed the minstrel. She noticed, although a bit too late, that his kiss was poison. It was but a spell that would force her to love him.

The minstrel thought the same and cursed himself for having fallen into her trap.

It was impossible for anyone to see the top of the staircase, which extended far above the clouds. The stairs took a different form each day: sometimes they were made of solid, hand-carved stone steps, other times of ice or of coal, and every so often, it was simply a rope ladder that led to nowhere in particular.

There was a pregnant woman, shivering from the cold and the uncertainty, who waited for days hoping that the stairs would adopt a more friendly form. She watched as the stairs transformed from sharpened, black volcanic rock to the fragile shards of a mirror, poised to break under the weight of her step. She watched as the stairs morphed into a ginormous vine with withered thorns crawling up its side.

She was repulsed by the idea of giving birth to the child of a man who had done her so much harm, though she did not dare take her own life. The only acceptable solution that she found was to climb the stairs from which nobody ever returned.

The steps of the stairs then transformed into a single, solid structure. They were now made of wood and velvet. The woman walked towards the stairs but, before she reached them, a hand grabbed her ankle.

"Not yet," said the dwarf. She too was pregnant, and in her eyes lived the same sadness.

"My grandfather told me that when he was a child, crickets used to be as small as his thumb," she said to her granddaughter. "And when I was a child, they couldn't even talk!"

III

Three of Doors

The Accordion Player

The music that flows from the beggar's accordion engraves itself, like an intense and lingering nightmare, in the minds of all those who do not spare him their coins. Those who do know that they are buying a bit of forgetfulness, which oddly feels like rest.

The people of the Barbs occupy the nests of birds long after they have gone. They have very few offspring, and almost all of them are old with age. They etch their names in the bark of the trees where the birds' nests lie, so that they may live longer.

The birds have every right to hate these spined creatures, as they spend their lives rushing the chicks, pushing them to grow independent, so that they leave the nest earlier than they should. The barbs are rugged, rude, and urticating, even when they caress each other with as much love as they are capable. But the birds do not hate them, quite the opposite, actually, because, with the death of each barb, a bird is born.

When he slid the ring onto his wife's finger, she screamed and writhed in pain. The metal band lost its shine and closed around her finger, tearing her flesh with its force.

Her husband, distressed at the sight, took too long before he finally understood. He then watched her gaze darken.

"You're not Catalina, are you?"

The creature shook its head. It meant to say no, that it was not this man's beloved bride, that it had taken her place, but the pain the creature felt did not allow for a single word to be said.

The ring closed around her finger tighter and tighter, until it was severed completely. The finger fell to the floor. Not a single drop of blood followed.

"Where is she?" asked the groom.

The creature, taking control of her body, picked up the finger and handed it to the groom. He accepted the offer, though perplexed. The nail was covered with cloudy marks and stains, which together painted the outline of his beloved's face, her eyes plagued with sorrow.

He turned to the imposter, hoping to meet its gaze, but it had gone.

The finger trembled ever so slightly in his palm.

IV

Four of Doors

The Name of the Guard

Many years had passed before she received the message. She needed to cross through that door to save her beloved, but beneath the threshold stood a guard, and he did not speak. She tried everything imaginable, but it was to no avail. She then asked his name. He opened his mouth and spoke the name of her beloved.

"That's not true," she said. "You are not he. I would have recognized him—I love him."

"If you truly loved me, you would have recognized me in this body. That was the door that you had to cross."

An artisan received notice of his impending death while he was working on a coffin. He refused to finish the commissioned piece, concluding that the tomb would soon belong to him. He sculpted along its border all that he would have liked to find in the Other World, and he cured the wood to protect it from woodworms.

A few days passed, and he was reincarnated into what artisans who venerate wood are typically reincarnated as: woodworms.

Each time that he needed a horse, he would light a bonfire and throw the branch of a gray tree into the burning flames. The smoke produced by the fire took the form of a steed, which he rode until his journey came to an end. The horse would then dissipate into a black cloud, ascending toward the sky.

He knew that he should not abuse the magic he was given, but he was ignorant of the risks, and did not know when to stop. Since nothing bad had ever happened, he decided to cast caution to the wind. It was then that the sky grew dark. An immense, dark cloud moved through the sky, galloping with the fury of a thousand angry beasts. The animals on the earth cowered at the sight.

He realized that with the storm came his punishment: the uncertainty of what might be.

AFTER MANY YEARS of simply observing the world, when the painter finally understood what they saw, his eyes swelled and matured, eventually falling to the ground, pulled by the gravity of their own weight. The baby, who waited silently at the painter's side, devoured them slowly.

V

Five of Doors

The countess was prepared to do whatever necessary to seduce the old king. She knew that the king spent all his time of late watching the pond where the naiads roamed, and so she decided to take advantage of his senile obsession.

She dyed her hair blue, plucked her eyelashes and eyebrows, sewed her fingers together, and pretended to have just emerged from the water. She knew that the king was to arrive shortly thereafter.

Her torso was one of the newest additions to the king's collection of hunting trophies.

The Bird that Bears the Night

His grandfather was very ill. The boy realized that the only way to save him was to prevent the break of dawn. With great effort, he managed to hold the sun below the horizon, but he then watched as all his beloved birds and all the other creatures shivered from the cold.

With tears in his eyes, the boy gave way to the rising sun. His grandfather's soul, grateful, was shaped like a blackbird.

The child was born with claws. The midwife, with her heart in a knot, told the mother that her son was stillborn. She ran through the rain to the cathedral, leaving the baby on its steps. She rang the bell and hid, waiting for someone to bring him in.

The door opened. The canon lifted the baby in his arms and gently positioned his claws against the cathedral's stone wall.

The child began to climb, despite the rain that soaked and shined the brick. The midwife watched as the gargoyles awaited his arrival.

THERE WAS A girl with the hands of a lizard. If one of her fingers was severed, another would grow in its place. She played the harp extraordinarily. Her mother warned her that she should take special care of her hands, since at any moment she could lose them (and the gift they gave her). But the girl ignored her mother's advice and instead designed a harp with strings so sharp they rang crystal-clear. Every theater invited her to perform. The prince of Bavaria announced that if the girl were truly a prodigy, he would marry her. The day of her most important performance, however, the girl with lizard hands became a woman, and so she lost her gift. Of course, she lost her fingers, too, which bled to the beat of her sorrow.

VI

Six of Doors

The Feathered Cat

When a cat grows a single feather, it can be used only to write a single story, and whatever story is written is guaranteed to be wonderful. The feather will then disappear. When a cat grows two feathers, each feather must be used to write a letter. When both letters are read, the feathers will disappear.

When a cat grows three feathers, it means that a baby girl will be born in the house to which the cat belongs. The cat need not be killed, nor the child. As time passes, the girl will turn into a woman, and those three feathers will turn into three blue birds. She will train two birds to be messengers, and the third she shall keep so that it may tell her its secret story.

When the three birds are reunited, no cat that is a cat will ever be born again.

It was said that good fortune would be given to those who touched the jester's hunchback, but that nine years of bad luck would be given to those who touched the hump of the beggar. So, the beggar decided to become a jester.

The ghost of the doe entered the room and threw herself over the hunter's wife, passing through her body. Nine months later, the matron fled the room where the hunter's wife had just given birth, overcome by a sudden wave of nausea. The hunter picked up the abomination and buried it in the forest.

It was then that the ghost finally abandoned the wife's body and went to stand watch over the grave of her son, who had finally been born.

When the doe arrived to where her child was buried, the fawn, in a vaporous state, rose from the ground and curled up in his mother's lap.

THE BOY KNEW that there were fictitious stories, and he knew that there were authentic ones. He could tell them apart because the authentic stories caused a chill to run up the nape of his neck. Very few stories, however, elicited such a response. The story of the Man of the Mist, for example, was authentic. He could sneak around the city without disturbing a single soul. The story of the capricious, yet kind-hearted Tooth Fairy, as well.

One night, despite the warmth provided by the weight of heavy blankets, the boy felt a chill in his toes, and he knew that the Man of the Mist had arrived. He shivered. He wanted to call for his mother but did not want to put her in danger. The boy felt the weight of two humid fingers, invisible to the eye, settle on his chest.

He then grabbed a glass from his nightstand and hit himself with enough force that one of his teeth fell loose. The room filled with the brilliance of a deep, blue light, and the Man of the Mist was frightened away.

VII

Seven of Doors

Her mother died. No other member of the household knew how to cook, and yet, the farmhouse would occasionally fill with the smell of freshly baked cookies.

At first, she was scared. But then she thought that she might be able to communicate with her mother through those smells. She planted a pot of her mother's favorite flowers. She left it in the kitchen, but it was to no avail.

She thought for a moment that maybe dead mothers preferred the smell of dead flowers, just as living mothers preferred the smell of living flowers. She went to the forest and picked a bunch of flowers, and she left them to wilt. That very afternoon she noticed the smell of freshly baked cookies.

White Animals

All white animals, with their gray or pink eyes, belong to the fairy queen. The ruler of the night, in turn, reigns over the insects so small that they seem to be nothing but a speck of dust, the beings shaped like branches or leaves, and all the creatures who have the power to confuse their prey.

Being as courteous as he is, the ruler of the night agrees to duel during the winter, on the snow-capped plains, when the queen's powers are at her strongest. And, being as courteous as she is, neither of them ever wins.

He returned to the village empty-handed, only to find that the other hunter had returned as well, the one who was competing against him for the reward. This other hunter had succeeded, carrying in his hands one of the beast's horns as proof of his feat.

The villagers told this hunter that a single horn was not enough, that they would not pay him the agreed amount. The beast could very well still be alive, even if she was missing a horn. They required the heart as proof. They planned to make a thick broth with it to comfort everyone and calm their fears of the beast.

Such was the hunter's determination that he returned to the place where he had killed the beast. Her corpse, however, was gone. The villagers, who knew beasts well, were right to have been so prudent, and the hunter understood that now.

He searched for the beast once more and found her with her horn still missing. The battle was fierce, and the hunter was lucky to have escaped with his life. He managed to defeat the beast once more, and this time, he made sure that she was dead. He sliced open her chest and dug through her insides to find her heart. He searched and searched, clawed and clawed, but simply could not find it. So, he skinned her. The weight of her bristly fur was almost too much to bear, and so he wore her skin like a cloak to better support it.

At dawn, the entire village watched from a safe distance how the first hunter killed the beast, the one that the other hunter had only managed to maim, and extracted the heart. Who would have guessed that the heart of a beast and the heart of a human were so similar? From the heart, a thick, thick broth was made. All the villagers tried it, and they were never again afraid of one another.

VIII

Eight of Doors

FROM THE ALMOND tree came fruit so delicious that nobody had ever managed to save a single seed to plant. This is why there only existed one almond tree. Each year, when the almonds matured, the entire town would gather in celebration of a great festival. That day, they would celebrate weddings, they would close business deals, and everyone felt as if they were friends with one other. It was said that the almonds had magical properties upon consumption, which was supposedly a secret zealously guarded by the people of the town.

Alisa saw the tree in bloom and wished, only for a moment, that its flowers would transform into fluttering butterflies. Alisa watched in astonishment as her wish came true. She then grew worried.

When her father found out what she'd done, he was so enraged that he hit her. Alisa climbed to the top of the almond tree, fearful of her father's reaction, and she wished with all her might that the butterflies would now become what they once had been.

At that moment, in thousands of places across the country, almond seeds fell to the ground. Many fortunately landed on fertile earth.

The Guiding Blackbird

HE KNEW THAT among all the blackbirds, there was one that could tell him where his mother had gone. So, he dragged the scarecrow into the barn, dressed in its clothes, and went to stand where it had stood.

Only one bird came to perch on his arm. It whispered:

"I will tell you what you wish to know if, in exchange, you let me peck at your eyes."

"But then I won't know in which direction to travel."

"Believe me, you won't need eyes to get to where you wish to go."

SHE KNEW THAT her son could see evil, which is why he avoided certain people. She always watched her son's reaction when she negotiated with others, or when she went to visit the Healer, or when they traveled. She sometimes wondered what it was that he saw. A color? A deformity? Some type of cloud or mist? They fled from all sorts of problems, and they did so at the slightest hint of evil. Her son's talent was quite useful, but it made him sadder with the passing of each day.

When the boy reached adolescence, he wished to see the world for himself. His mother would not allow it: "You have no idea of the dangers you could face," she would tell him. The boy began to act strange every time he saw his reflection in the mirror. It was much too late before his mother realized that he was beginning to hate himself. The boy took his own life with a piece of broken glass.

His mother tried to imagine what he could have seen as he looked in that mirror for the last time, though it was now shattered and covered in blood. She stared and stared at the mirror, refusing to move until she understood what her son could have possibly seen, what could possibly have driven him to do such a thing.

And then she saw it. It was not a color or deformity, nor was it a cloud. It was something more profound than pain, more profound than what she had always assumed. She saw herself, just as she was. Her son did not, could not, stand the monster she was. And so, she did just as her mother had always taught her to do. She ran from the evil.

She turned away from the image in the mirror so that she no longer had to contemplate her true form: that of a mother who did not allow her child to live, but who instead let him die.

IX

Nine of Doors

The lumberjack who saved the girl from the wolf visited her house every day with a bouquet of flowers to reap his reward, which was the girl's hand in marriage. Every day his bouquets grew bigger, every day he sat closer to the door, and every day he looked more and more like the wolf.

The Stone that Awaits You

You place your hand on top of the great, split stone: Legend says that hidden in its cracks and crevices is the wisdom of the animal kingdom. You think about all the winters that must have passed to create a crack like that, all the rain, all the ice…

Suddenly, you see the stone open its eye, and you realize that the crack is not a crack, but a mouth whose teeth have just clamped around your hand.

When a faun loses his voice (which is something that happens quite frequently), his throat transforms into a dragonfly and flies off. Only if a real dragonfly mistakes the faun's dragonfly as one of its own will the faun recover his voice. He'll no longer need to steal the voice of some human child.

The queen's taster was in love with her. He dreamed of the moment in which he would confess his love for her, with his final breath, in the throes of death, and after having saved her life in a heroic act. But the queen was also in love with the taster, and so she would taste a bite of every food before he arrived. If he died, she would have no desire to live.

They never had the chance to speak with one another. Neither knew how the other felt.

Convinced that his love for the queen would never be requited, the taster decided to poison himself so that he might finally have the chance to sing to the queen the beautiful words that he spent years planning. And so, he did.

Neither the queen nor the taster died that day, however. The taster declared his love for the queen, believing that those would be his last words; the queen then kissed him, and they ran off together. There are rumors that the merchant who sold the poison was also in love with the taster. Once he learned of the taster's plan, or possibly having believed that the taster was going to kill the queen, the merchant gave the taster a harmless potion to spare him of such a fate. Others say that the merchant was none other than the king in disguise. And, well, there are those who say that true love, or words of love, or even kisses, are a type of antidote. Lastly, there are some who say that what truly saved the taster was simply the great tolerance his body had developed to all types of poisons.

X

Boy of Doors

Drops of Water

He noticed that the white flowers, once picked, would transform into drops of dew if he took his eyes off them, even if for just a moment. So, he did everything possible to keep his eyes fixed on the bouquet of white flowers that he carried. He hoped to give the bouquet to his grandmother. However, he blinked just as he was arriving home, and the flowers turned into water droplets sitting on the stems.

The boy began to cry, having failed to bring the flowers to his grandmother. She wiped away his tears with her thumb, and in her hand a flower bloomed.

The stained-glass window depicted two cats fighting furiously. When someone asked the priest about its meaning, he often responded by saying that it was a metaphor for Strongfield's famous diatribe, or that it was a symbolic representation of two prophets in disagreement. He never spoke of its true meaning, which had been revealed to him by one of the cats. The black one.

Along the path, she came across an old woman who seemed about to choke, and so she offered her all the water she had.

The old woman composed herself and said:

"Thank you for the water. Without it, I would not have been able to complete my task today."

"And what is your task?"

"I am Death, and today I must take with me a woman whose ear is torn."

The woman covered her ear with her hair.

FAIRIES CAN ONLY live in the dark. If light is ever to touch them, they turn into monsters. That is why they are impossible to see.

But the boy wanted so badly to see the fairies that he entered the cave anyway, holding in his hand a very small candle, the same one that they had placed on his birthday cake. He was certain that this would not harm any magical creature.

He walked further into the cave and was met only with silence.

He then heard a subtle rustle, and his heart skipped a beat. He was finally about to see a fairy!

An avalanche of bats loomed over the boy, blowing out his candle. He realized, just a little too late, that he had killed all the fairies.

XI

Maid of Doors

The Girl Behind the Open Door

She knew that she was a monster because she did not have eyelids. Instead, she had scales. Nobody else had seemed to notice. Fortunately, her scales were identical to human eyelids.

But she knew they were scales.

She dreamt that night that she could make a carriage capable of transporting her anywhere in the world. Horses were expensive, but doves could belong to anyone who could catch and care for them. The doves that she had caught had chicks, and those chicks had never been free, so they never learned to fly. The carriage worked wonderfully as a traditional carriage, but unlike in her dreams, the carriage never managed to take flight. Just as she made the decision to let her birds go free, they took flight, drawing the carriage toward the clouds, faster than she had ever dreamed.

A boy imagined the beginning of a story, but he could not think of an ending. So as to not forget this budding tale, he attached a tiny silver bell to his ankle.

The boy aged and became a troubadour. He never removed the bell, hoping that time would reveal to him the ending of the story he had created as a mere child. Each time that he thought of another detail, the bell grew. Eventually, it reached the size of a nut, and then an apple. Even though the story progressed in his head like the shade of a growing tree, it was impossible for the boy to determine its ending. The weight of the bell was becoming too much.

When the bell reached the size of a watermelon, the troubadour decided that he would no longer travel from town to town. He would have to wait until after he found the ending to his story. He untied the bell from his ankle, placed it on the floor, and sat in front of it so that he could finally just think.

On the surface of the silver bell, the boy saw his reflection. He saw his oblong features, deformed by the curvature of the bell, and for a moment, it mimicked the round cheeks and smooth skin he had had as a child.

It was then that he realized the end of his story could be found at the beginning. After decades, he returned to the town where he was born, and he saw that the girl he had loved as a boy was now a widow. The bell then grew just a bit more, until it transformed into a cradle.

XII

Jack of Doors

Every stone used to build the witch's cabin rolled down the mountain until it found the precise spot where it belonged. Each branch of heather used to construct the roof was carried gently by the wind until it reached the place where it was destined to be.

Well, at least that is how the little girl had dreamed the cabin was built—a girl who, when she awoke, decided that she wanted to be a witch.

A true witch has no cabin. It is of no use to her, as she does not sleep. She spends her nights going from town to town, blowing sweet dreams over little girls as they sleep.

They were given a stew made of chickpeas to help feed the orphans. Floating on top was a single black chickpea, which the nun removed so that none of the children would have to eat it. Since she didn't like to waste food, she decided to eat it herself. She then became ravenous and decided that the stew was too delicious for the children. She devoured it all.

The following day, the nun died between convulsions. As she closed her eyes for the last time, from her mouth popped out a tiny black chickpea.

The priest examined the bean closely. It smiled at him, its tiny mouth full of sharpened teeth.

The Goldsmith's Apprentice

He crafted a bell that, when rung, sounded like a child's laugh. All the townsfolk admired his work, but his teacher did not let him finish his studies quite yet.

"I will not let you leave until you've created something that stretches the limits of your talent."

The apprentice thought that his teacher was mocking him, and so he made a bell that imitated the laugh of an old man.

Satisfied, the teacher allowed his apprentice to go.

"The path to the devil can start a thousand different ways, but it only ends in one," said the grandmother to her granddaughter when she offered her a basket of black strawberries. She forced her granddaughter to burn them in the fireplace.

Her grandmother explained that in the depths of the forest, there sat two strawberry bushes, one pure and the other treacherous. The latter produces a black fruit that corrupts everything it touches, while the former discerns those of pure heart and helps them along their journey.

The girl did not dare tell her grandmother that the strawberries were red before she first picked them and that they turned black the moment she touched them.

XIII

Sage of Doors

The Queen Bee

The young prince spent much of his time observing the bees.

"Mother, if you are queen, doth that mean you have granted life to all the members of the court?"

The queen smiled.

"Of course not, my dear. But to thee alone."

The boy left the room, and the queen finally removed the corset that hid her breasts. She was relieved that the rest of her children were not quite as clever.

~

She always tried to decipher the complex messages left on the window by the ice lord. She suspected that he had been in love with her for years and that he was waiting for her to reach an appropriate age.

It was summer the day that she turned ninety years old, but she found the window covered in an intricate pattern of frozen crystals. She understood his message and climbed the mountain with a smile spread across her cheeks.

~

The witches' apprentice saw a man's face in the bowl of sparrow's blood. One of her teachers told her, "That is the face of your beloved." The other warned her that it was the face of certain death.

The apprentice took a deep breath. She knew what her teachers had meant to say, that a witch can only have one daughter, that this daughter would inherit her mother's powers, and that her mother would inevitably die while giving birth.

While at the tavern, she saw the man whose face she had seen drawn in the bowl of sparrow's blood a month prior. He was a traveler, just passing through. At that moment, she realized that she was no longer an apprentice but a true witch, and she decided that she too was a traveler, just passing through.

SHE KNEW THAT the insects floating on the surface of the lake were actually the spirits of stillborn children. Nobody had explained this to her, but when her mother lost the baby, one of those insects suddenly appeared in the bath where she was bathing after her delivery. The girl was scared that the baby might try to crawl back into her mother's body and make her sad again, and so she grabbed the spirit of her sister and squished it in her palm until it no longer moved.

XIV

Elder of Doors

The witch gave the prince one of the wings of the Baleful Bird. She told him to keep it in the pocket of his suit and to ensure that it never leaves his side.

"If the two wings are ever reunited, the monster will be reborn. The other wing, however, lives on the other side of the world."

The prince nodded.

Years later, the witch died. The prince, who was now king, was tired of always carrying that sinister object, and so he left it abandoned in a room.

The queen found those beautiful feathers and ordered that a hat be made from them, so that she might wear it while visiting distant countries across the ocean.

The Stone King

Each morning, the old man sits on a stone, his crown of elder and illera resting on his head. Majestic, he waits for his subjects to come to him seeking either council or justice. Nobody ever comes, and yet, the sounds of the Deep Forest are dampened slightly. Where he sits, no one has ever found a nest in the ground or a bloodstained rabbit.

On his way back from a hunting trip, the bartender discovered that the blood of the whitewing had intoxicating properties. He set out to capture and bleed as many whitewings as he could. He then began to sell their blood under the guise of an exotic liquor, as if it were from a foreign land.

The drink was a success, and the bartender grew rich. Men from all regions of the forest came to try it. Some said that they dreamt of whitewings whenever they drank that wonderful liquor.

Each night, the bartender went out to hunt. And each day, he had fewer and fewer clients.

THERE IS A woman who fears that she might turn into a cat. She does not sleep very well. She tries to sleep through the night, hoping to avoid the habits of the very creature that she fears, but her anxieties keep her from resting. During the day, she is so fatigued that she simply cannot carry on.

There is a woman who fears that she might turn into a cat, and she is afraid of mice. Or at least that's what she tries to tell herself when she hunts them, compulsively.

She can't stand the water. She has grown so accustomed to the darkness of the night that she can see perfectly without light. She eats only meat, and only a few times a day. And, occasionally, she feels the irresistible urge to uproot and nibble some herbs.

Every day she repeats to herself, terrified, that what scares her most in the world is to turn into something so different from herself.

Chapter 4: Hearths

I

Ace of Hearths

The Girl of Dreams, who had grown until she was no longer a girl, walked and walked until she reached the glass coffin in which the Boy of Thorns slept. Standing there, she saw a young girl who observed him with loving eyes.

"I can't find the courage to kiss him," confessed the girl. "I don't want to die."

"Don't worry, my dear," said the Girl of Dreams. "I will do it for you."

The Girl of Dreams gently kissed the Boy of Thorns and fell into the glass coffin to take his place. She grew younger and more youthful as new thorns began to sprout.

The Little Flame

"Only something quite small will be able to save you," said the witch.

The wounded woman searched through anthills, she tried every flower, she let herself be bitten by fleas and tiny house spiders.

But nothing could cure her. She was so ill that even her lunar cycle had stopped. Could there be a more certain prelude to death than that?

That night, she had a dream. A small being had grown in her stomach, and it told her, with tears in its eyes, that it could only cure her if she forgot of its existence. In her dream, she accepted.

The following day, her cycle returned. She wondered what she was doing so far from home, and so she returned, having forgotten that she was ever sick.

The count's son was so beautiful that the entire world, all except one person, thought that he always told the truth. Old women held him in high esteem, as they would a grandson, and old men thought that any rumors about him simply came from jealous children.

However, the count's son was not good. He preyed on girls until he withered away their prudence, and after he made love to them three or four times, he would no longer speak to them, threatening them with death if they did not remain silent. He himself even drowned many of his newborn children.

The daughter of the swineherd was the prettiest of the village and as tall and strong as the boys. She had always resisted the advances of the count's son. The night that he tried to have his way with her, she slit his throat without a second thought, just as she did with the swine.

She sat, frightened of what she had just done, and realized that if her crime were to be discovered, neither she nor her family would live to tell the tale. So, she carefully carved around his face and made a mask from the skin. She bound her chest and practiced speaking in his tone of voice the entire afternoon. Then, she walked to the palace, ready to pass as the son of the count.

The count, who was the only person who had known the truth about his son, observed her for a while. He heard her words, calm and kind. He noticed the color of her eyes, slightly different from usual. Relieved, the count never told anybody that the person standing in front of him was not his son.

> The girl was certain that she had caught a star and refused to open her hands for weeks. She barely slept, and when she did, she asked her sister to bind her hands together so that the star could not escape its enclosure. When she thought that nobody was watching, she would cry from the pain, from the heat that scorched her hands. Yet she refused to let the star go.

II

Two of Hearths

The roasted lamb that rested on the table had the exact same look in its eyes as her dead son. She decided to never again eat roasted lamb.

She noticed that same look in the eyes of the broiled hare, the grilled trout, and even the stuffed quail.

She really shouldn't have eaten her son. It had ruined her appetite forever.

The queen knew that the evil sorcerer, anguished in the face of her rejection, had transformed her daughter into a flower. She scoured the forest, day and night, in search of a flower, any flower, that bore a resemblance to her child, though she was quite careful not to step on a single one. She knew that only tears provoked by true pain would bring her daughter back.

One night, leaning against the trunk of a tree and exhausted from the tears she spilled over every potential match, the queen fell asleep. She woke just in time to see a mother wolf cry over the loss of her own daughter. She watched as the wolf's tears spilled over the most beautiful flower of them all, transforming it into a small pup.

The champion of the realm went to seek help from the elder warrior, serene victor of innumerable battles.

"What must I do to become an invincible, undefeatable paladin?" the champion asked with his chin to his chest as a sign of respect.

The veteran waited quite a while before he answered.

"You must stay so still that the vine of the maiden grape can curl around your feet and grow up your legs."

As he spoke those words, he lifted his tunic, showing his leg and the thick veins that crawled up his side.

The champion had not expected such advice, but he accepted it anyway. He stood as still as a statue through rain, thirst, and thunder, until the grapevine had conquered his left leg, marking him with her painful tendrils and petite suckers.

"Now, you are invincible," promised the veteran, freeing the champion's leg with the slightest, yet astonishingly complicated, movement of his dagger.

The champion of the realm understood and went to sit next to his elder by the fire. He knew that he would never again step foot on a battlefield.

He Who Sketches the Wolves

"He knows to draw nothing else," whispered his mother.

The guests observed the boy as he sat in the corner. He stared at a fixed point in front of him as he rapidly sketched lines and shapes. When they inched closer to see what he had drawn, they found the perfect image of a ghastly, terrifying wolf. It had piercing white eyes and a gaping maw. Black saliva dripped from its fangs.

One of the guests tried to conceal her gasp and muttered, terrified, "It's almost as if the fangs were right in front of him."

Another guest saw a drop of ink fall, staining the page. Near the boy, however, there was nothing that even closely resembled a jar of pigment.

III

Three of Hearths

THE MAP MAKER traverses the forest, and along the way, she lays out rope and uses the length of her strides to measure the shadows. Her goal is to define definitively which areas of the forest are the most terrible and dangerous. She plans to mark where they begin and where they end, so that she may warn all those who come near.

She tries her best to avoid the most dangerous parts of the forest because, well, who else would finish the map? So, she carries on her back a cage with the tiniest, most trusting animals. She lures them in with a handful of seeds and nuts by the calm clearings of the forest. If she suspects danger, she simply throws a rabbit towards the entrance of a dark cave, or the hollowed trunk of a tree, and then she can calculate just how long it takes for the creature to be devoured, struck down, or vaporized.

The Flower of Flames

THE MAIDEN TRIED to pluck the blazing flower from the earth, but she burned her hand. The knight tried to slice the flower with his sword, but the sword was reduced to ashes. It was then that a young girl blew gently on the flower, as if she were blowing out a candle, and the wisps transformed into petals.

THE PRINCESS HEARD others talk about the heart, and she thought it to be the cause of her misfortunes. She hid where nobody could find her, unbuttoned her dress, and gently lifted the skin that covered her chest to reveal a small robin in a white cage. Its song was hauntingly beautiful, but with each note, the princess suffered.

So, she took the robin from its cage, and in its place she put a black crow.

The robin flew until it reached the market, and it landed above the flower merchant's post. He recognized the robin immediately.

Weeks later, the princess celebrated her marriage to the ruler of a neighboring kingdom. Halfway through the wedding ceremony, an enormous female crow struck the princess, ripping the skin off her chest, so that her husband could be freed from his prison.

The merchant brought the robin closer to the princess's deserted body, but it refused to enter its cage. Quicker than a spark of lightning, the robin flew into the merchant's mouth, and it never left.

IV

Four of Hearths

The Darkest of Doors

The tiny red herb (the one shaped like a trident) is dangerous. If you step on it and it pokes your bare foot, you might not even notice, but your foot will then belong to the lord of the underworld.

You'll begin to walk in circles without understanding why. Then, one night, one of your feet will tear off the other. The one that remains shall carry you, with terrible hops, to the darkest of doors.

He placed a firefly in his mouth, just for a brief instant, so that it would fly free the moment he declared his love for her. But the firefly kept flying, and it flew down his throat and into the depths of his core, ultimately sacrificing its life.

When she saw him arrive, she said, "Oh, how brightly your heart shines!"

And she loved him forever.

The duke killed his enemy. As his enemy breathed his last breath, out came a terrible wind that closed itself around the duke, keeping him from walking in the direction that he wished to go.

The wind pushed him toward the lost moor. He struggled and struggled. Along the way, he lost his sword, his hat, and all the decor that adorned his garb. The duke listened to his intuition, and he knew not to open his mouth. It was crucial that he keep it shut.

Never did there exist an enemy as furious as this rampant gale, bereft of the body from which it came and whose strength was not easy to master. A powerful gust of wind managed to pry open the duke's mouth, allowing all the air to rush inside. After that, the wind simply became breath once again.

UNICORNS ARE NOT visible to everyone. Even in certain moments, when all who are present can see and identify the exact spot in which the unicorn stands, each person describes it differently. "It has two small wings," says the baker. "No, that can't be," says the traveling merchant, "its most striking feature is its long, black mane." "No, no, its mane is white," argues the girl, "and it has two tails." "There are no tails," retorts the baker, "but instead of hooves…"

Every time a unicorn makes itself visible, it becomes the center of an argument.

Unicorns cannot be seen by everyone. They remain invisible to those who have a peaceful spirit.

V

Five of Hearths

He Who Dresses the Gods

He travels from church to church with his splendid cloths, multicolored wings, brass spokes and halos, and he speaks for hours with the priests, monks, and druids to decide which attire will best represent their gods.

It is not always as easy as it seems. Quite often, not even the priests themselves can come to an agreement about which traits should be used to describe the Creator, the Mother, and the spirits.

The tailor, although he caters to the gods, does not believe in a single one. He only believes in the outfits he creates.

The two sisters lived very far from each other, but they found a magical way to communicate using two prodigious cups. Whatever liquid was poured into one of the cups would instantly appear in the other. They had always kept this wonder hidden from their husbands. One sister was happily married, while the other had only agreed to marriage because she felt a sense of obligation. Her husband was insufferable and despotic.

Every day, the sisters surprised each other with small gifts: honeysuckle tea, gooseberry wine, a bit of mead. They celebrated anniversaries and achievements together, toasting to their health and happiness.

One day, however, one of the cups did not get filled. And, a few days after that, one sister received news that the other had died and that her husband was accused of poisoning her. She realized quickly that it was her own husband who had tried to poison her. And all those years that she had pretended to love him, well, they turned into centuries.

WHATEVER HE HAD fished out of the water was not a fish. It had the eyes of a fish, yes, and the scales. It was slimy. But its body was shaped like that of a human child.

The creature began to cry when it was pulled from the water. The fisherman looked at it, feeling both repulsion and affection toward the creature. He realized that if he were to adopt the creature, he could no longer be a fisherman. But then how could he make a living? He would have to renounce that which gave him independence, changing his lifestyle completely.

He brought the child to his wife and shared his worries with her. She looked him in the eyes, serious, and said:

"That's what love is."

VI

Six of Hearths

"MAYBE THAT PEA was too small," said the queen.

So, she tried again with a chickpea, a hazelnut, a walnut, an early potato, a turnip, and eventually a small pumpkin. The day that the queen placed an enormous watermelon under the princess's mattress, and the princess was still not disturbed, was when she finally noticed how the princess's hands were ever so slightly translucent.

The Sleeping Bear

AS HE SWALLOWED the last bite of wild peach, he noticed that the pit was shaped like a tiny, sleeping bear. Without giving it much thought, he gave the pit to his son to play with.

"Papa, the bear woke up!" exclaimed the boy. But his father, as usual, paid him no mind.

The following morning, the boy was gone. There were footprints as big as a bear's that trailed from the entrance of the house down to the forest, where the wild peaches grew.

THERE EXISTS A magic horn that, from a distance, mimics the rustling of the leaves as they move in the forest. A boy, whose diet consisted only of flowers, found the horn one afternoon, and he held it gently against his ear. From that moment on, he knew he would not be able to rest until he found that marvelous place.

There are very few jobs more dangerous than that of the feather collector. Most of his time is spent climbing the tallest trees in the forest, and so he often forgets how to live like those who keep their feet on the ground. That is why, when he confessed his love to the woman he'd chosen, offering her his most beautiful treasures, she barely understood him, and she certainly didn't understand how truly beautiful his feathers were. She wasn't interested in his stories about the brittlebird, who sleeps for decades in the trunks of trees; or the dangerous Stone Goose, who, upon death, will turn to marble and fall from the sky just as a meteor does, causing inexplicable deaths; or the Whispering Kingfisher, who enjoys confusing those in love. Women hardly ever listen to the feather collector.

But, when the feather collector climbs to the top of the oldest cypress tree in the cemetery and, there, just as the morning dew forms, hears the song of the newborn owlets, he need not think about anything else.

VII

Seven of Hearths

The Other Side of the Door

"When I leave, do not open this door under any circumstances," said her stepmother, who only adopted little girls.

The girl promised. But, given that she was both obedient and curious, she convinced her best friend that he should be the one to open the door.

Once open, she saw her stepmother, who was now an ogre, waiting with her mouth open wide. She devoured the girl's friend in a single bite.

Boys, however, were poison.

She dreamed that her body was covered in white beetles and that their armor felt like velvet to the touch. They danced along her skin for some time. They would find an orifice, always the same one, and disappear inside. When she woke, she wondered if that orifice meant something. She wondered if it was the place through which she should sink her dagger, in hopes of erasing her memories, of destroying any potential she had to love. She wished more than anything to forget he who had been her lover, but she did not want to risk her life.

One night, under the soft glow of the moon, she saw one of those beetles. Awake, she followed it through the forest as fast as her legs could carry her, and she arrived at a clearing, though mist shrouded her view. As she breathed in the aroma, she felt an instant joy. She let the mist pass through her body, through the very same orifice as in her dreams. It dissolved all the pain that she felt, both past and future.

THERE IS A palace made of books, and many say that it belongs to a tyrant. They say he wants to paralyze the power of words, condemning each book to eternal silence and reducing its purpose to that of a mere brick.

There are others, however, who say that the palace was built by a generous benefactor. They say that he hopes to conserve those books for centuries, sparing them from any misfortunes, so that future generations may enjoy the words they hold inside.

Finally, there are some who try to convince you that these books have ghosts and that, as you approach the palace, the ghosts whisper in your ear the scenes they lived and the dialogues they spoke, carving them into your memory forever, sending chills up your spine.

> THE PRINCESS FORGOT to carry with her the keys to the secret passageway, and when she returned, she was locked out of the palace. She ran to the front gate with the hope that the guards would let her in, but when she told them who she was, they simply scoffed, incredulous. The princess was insistent, however, and so the guards brought her before the queen.
>
> The widowed queen declared with a kind smile that she had no idea who that girl was, though she offered her work as a palace servant, if the girl so desired.
>
> The princess realized that this was a punishment designed by her stepmother. The maids whom the princess had scorned and taunted so many times simply looked at her and laughed.

VIII

Eight of Hearths

He could not help but seduce all the women who crossed his path. One woman, jealous of the others, disguised herself as a man so that she could seduce them first and keep them from her beloved.

What the man could not figure out was why his beloved went to such lengths to seduce all the women who crossed her path. That is why he did the same.

She Who Sculpts the Flame

Nobody has ever seen a still flame. However, those who admire certain sculptures made of red wood instantly recognize their shape.

When they ask the sculptor how she could possibly sculpt that which nobody has seen, she explains that she can only look at the flame once a day, after she wakes in the morning, and after the darkness of the night has healed her eyes once again.

The best customers, those who pay the most, are the dwarfs, which is why the artist started creating his paintings on a smaller canvas.

Financial circumstances changed, favoring the wind sprites. The artist exchanged his already tiny paintbrushes for some that were even tinier and began to paint his pieces on silver coins.

He was quite old by the time the wise grasshoppers desired his portraits. His brushes were now made of nothing more than two or three very fine strands of hair from the mane of a unicorn, a material somewhat like silk. He created these paintings on the surface of a pumpkin seed, flat and round.

As he neared the end of his life, when his eyes were worn and tired, he received a visit from the smallest client of them all: the fairy queen.

THERE ONCE WERE two sisters, one beautiful and the other happy. The happy one was visited every day by a bird, and this bird would give her exactly one gold coin. The beautiful one could see the eyes of ghosts floating in the air, small and translucent as they were, and it is why her own were so deep and mysterious, and her skin so pale.

The beautiful sister never knew what to do with her beauty, much less the sorrow she felt as she contemplated the despair and damnation of these ghosts, ghosts with which she could not communicate. The happy sister could have been sad, but she was not, precisely because she never once wondered about the bird and the coins he brought her.

IX

Nine of Hearths

If taken properly, wise herb will increase your intelligence for about an hour. But if you abuse it, you will either go insane or blind. Some who take wise herb are not afraid of blindness, but they are afraid of insanity. For others, it's just the opposite. Only those who fear neither blindness nor insanity can fully realize the effects of the herb: to be one with the herb, to allow their mind to open, to reach a state of true enlightenment in which sight and sanity are nothing more than a distraction.

The Sick Bird

She cradled the sick bird in the palm of her hands, watching, feeling, as it died. She felt an ache in her chest as Death climbed from her hands to her arms and into her heart. She realized at that moment that her grandfather was not simply traveling and that she would never see him again.

The dead bird opened its beak and uttered a single word that the girl did not understand. When she repeated the word, her mother burst into tears.

There are two staircases, one for those who ascend and one for those who descend. The staircases are intertwined, spiraling around one another.

Our capes are full of secret folds, crevices, and pockets: some fold inward, while others fold outward, and in them we hide such things as love letters.

We climb the staircase every day at the very same hour, at the very same time. We never see each other because you ascend while I descend, but I hear footsteps that I know are yours, and you hear mine. If it were not so, then why do we stop on the same stair? How could we press our hands together against the alabaster wall, so thin that sometimes your warmth reaches mine, until the rush of footsteps from above and below pushes us to go our separate ways?

Each night, separated from our bodies by a thin wall of fabric, one that still lets the warmth pass through, these love letters become our hands.

> "IF YOU SAY my name," said the grotesque creature, "I will grant you one wish."
>
> She thought about his offer for a moment.
>
> "If I knew your name," she replied, "I could tell it to all my loved ones, and they would share it with all of theirs. They would all come to you asking for their wishes to be granted, and in doing so, some would share their most secret, selfish, and even vengeful desires, and surely their desires cannot all come true at once, surely many are simply incompatible…"
>
> The creature smiled in such a way that the girl knew she had solved its riddle. Its smile grew even wider when it noticed the spark in her eyes, the clarity. She bit her lips.
>
> "Your name is Contention," the girl blurted out. "And my wish is to forget of your existence and to forget that this conversation ever happened."
>
> As a look of disappointment spread across its face, the creature vanished into thin air.

X

Boy of Hearths

It took him quite a while to realize that demons were small and aquatic, and that they did not live in a person's heart like he thought, but in their eyes, which turned blue as a sign of possession.

The demons were much more vulnerable than they seemed; they would burst, bloody, after being hit just right, and so he was not afraid.

The Soul

"Each snowflake, as it falls, is actually an angel's soul, separated from its body by the cold. They lay still during the winter, watching what happens here on the earth, and in the spring, as the air warms, their souls turn into dew and return to heaven."

The boy smiled, relieved. It meant that during the summer, nobody had been watching.

He could recognize the song of every bird. He could distinguish with absolute accuracy the males from the females, the young from the old.

This is why, when he heard the song of a bird that he did not recognize, it woke him immediately from his sleep. He peered out the window in an attempt to spot the bird that made that noise, but all he saw was the darkness of the night. So, he kept listening. He imagined a bird in his mind: the shape of its beak, the color of its feathers, the look of its tail, the way that it spread its wings in preparation for flight.

The next morning, he saw, though only for a moment, the bird that he had imagined, flying silently through the sky. It was magnificent; it looked nothing like any bird he had seen in that region before. He was amazed by how similar reality was to his imagination.

Then, a boy walked past the front of his house, whistling as he went. It was the song sung the night before. He looked back to the sky, but the bird was gone.

THE WITCH ACCEPTED her death, and when she touched the flame, she disintegrated into an endless slurry of salamanders. As they dispersed, they left the floor covered in tiny, black footprints. Each one of these salamanders traveled toward a person that the witch had known in life. Some salamanders brought prosperity, warming the house, the kitchens and the bathrooms, keeping the bitter cold out. Other salamanders searched for the most prized possessions of certain individuals and burned them to ashes.

One of these salamanders, just one, crawled into the bed of a sleeping man and laid down on his chest. The man's skin was cold because he had just died. The salamander restored the warmth to his chest, and the man woke, frightened. He had dreamt terrible things: that the woman he had loved sacrificed herself for him.

XI

Maid of Hearths

She Who Sells Cosmetics

The best publicity for her merchandise is her own beauty. The merchant of powders and perfumes has skin like that of a little girl. She has the curious mouth of an adolescent, the wise eyes of a wife, the round, full cheeks of a mother, and the slim, serene body of an older woman.

Under the layers of makeup, it's impossible to know what her eyebrows first looked like, or her lips. Her face is a blank canvas, one that she paints again and again, day after day, adding, combining, creating, color over color.

When she is alone, her obsessions consist of quite the opposite. Aware that she is simply a medium through which beauty is performed, she eliminates her features. She blurs them and destroys them.

The duke's son was in want of a playmate, and so he sewed together a leather doll. One night, he dreamt that the wind carried a single Redflower seed and placed it in the doll's throat.

The boy searched the entire forest for the Redflower, and after several weeks, he finally found it. He then had to wait until the flower turned into a crimson fruit, and then again until that fruit produced its singular seed. He then slit the doll's throat and placed the seed inside.

From that night on, he dreamt that the doll spoke to him of the marvelous country of the free beings, of creatures made of cloth and string, where nobody was alone. The doll even told him what magical words he should say, and how to do it.

Now, slitting his own throat was a bit more difficult, but the seed fit perfectly.

THE RIFTS ONLY have one eye, a very tiny one, though they have no use for it. In their kingdom of textures and cracks and crevices, light is simply an unnecessary distraction. Yet, newborn infants still conserve this annoying feature quite stubbornly. It is from an era long since passed in which the Rifts lived outdoors.

The eyes of these elves are the most vulnerable parts of their bodies, as a single drop of brezuhur sap in their eye is enough to kill one individual and all his closest relatives. Perhaps that is why they never open their eyes.

Those who live in the kingdom of the Rifts, once known for their moving paintings, now hide. They bury themselves and flee deep into the earth. They wish to know nothing.

XII

Jack of Hearths

The Beast at Her Feet

The daughter of the farmer entered the castle. The servants took her coat and told her that she must remove her shoes if she is to walk on the carpet, which was so thick that it reached her ankles. The carpet was reminiscent of a field of wheat, brushed by the wind, and it welcomed her bare feet, surrounding them with the warmth of a living creature.

"And where is the beast?" she asked, her voice fearful.

The servants lowered their gaze.

The savior of toys travels with his wagon from house to house. He knocks, and when the door opens, he unfurls his carpet, placing down boxes of toys: bees made of velvet, theaters for mice made of plush, balloons that ascend when the candle inside is lit.

He asks for no money, but rather old toys, dolls of cloth and hay that were sewn with love. No one understands how those dolls, tarnished from age, could possibly be worth as much as the stunning creations of velvet and metal that he offers in exchange.

The artisan, when alone, devours these toys drenched in time and uses the massive amount of energy that they provide to prolong his life even more, century after century. It will never cease to amaze him that people prefer those shiny trinkets to objects that carry so many emotions, so many memories, simply because the trinkets are new.

Hiccups are the language spoken by the creatures of the air. With each hiccup, with something so little, we say so much. If only we knew how to understand the words we express, we would never need another piece of advice.

Because Arina was the daughter of one of these creatures of the air, she was able to understand. When she walked by someone as they hiccupped, she would transcribe the message she heard onto a piece of paper and leave it nearby, though careful to make sure no one saw her. Because she was the daughter of one of these creatures and a human, and because others did not approve of such a union, her parents and their descendants were punished. And so, Arina never got the hiccups.

There was a day, a moment, when she felt the urge to flee the forest. In desperate need of advice, she asked the local peddler for help. She knew well that the creatures of the air did not like that hiccups were traded or bartered, but there were many things that they did not like.

"I want you to sell me some hiccups," she said.

The peddler stared at her.

"For you or for someone else?" he replied.

"For me."

He shook his head.

"It'll cost you. And you wouldn't even know what to do with them."

The peddler gave her a bout of hiccups, and to conserve them, he pulled from his satchel a cage made of bones from several creatures of the air.

The girl, horrified, realized that advice given by these creatures was not something to be bought on a whim, and she killed the murderer of her people with her bare hands.

At once, she was given the gift of the hiccup.

XIII

Sage of Hearths

The Healer of Birds

The girl, instead of dying, turned into a swan. The priest knew not if this was a miracle performed by the goddess or the work of devils, and so he caged the swan to investigate. He found no evidence on her exterior, and so he had to dig deeper. He searched and searched until he found what he was looking for.

From that moment on, the priest could take the wings of any injured bird and make them capable of flight once more. Many saw this as a divine gift, but the priest knew that it was nothing more than a small compensation for the loss of his soul.

"The drops of rain that fall from the sky are angels' tears," they told him. He thought, then, that perhaps these holy tears could do away with the demons that laid siege to the city. He waited until the sky was full of gray clouds, and the clouds full of rain. With the help of many men, he dug a channel from the surface of the earth down to the pits of Hell, exposing it to the elements.

The rain began to shower, but it fell no further than the channel's entrance. The heat evaporated the angels' tears before they could go any further.

A cacophony of laughter rose from the depths of the pit, inflammable, like gas as it burns. The men simply shrugged their shoulders and inched closer to warm themselves.

Some trees do not know what they are, and so they think that they'll be able to pull their roots from the ground and walk to the banks of the river, discovering new soils and new birds in the process. As their bodies harden, however, these trees soon learn that their dream will never come true.

Despite their immobility, they never forget their wish. They never resign themselves to their condition. Their roots extend and extend, far past the perimeter of the forest, until they reach the depths of the earth, warmed by its touch. They explore the cultivated lands, the houses of men, women, and children, bearing witness to all their impulses and sins.

To know, to feel the dreams of both humans and animals is consolation enough for not having been able to achieve their own. When their roots reach Hell, they realize that every inhabitant is there because of a dream they once had.

XIV

Elder of Hearths

There exists a plant with lusciously warm petals whose flowers are shaped like lips. It is said that when someone with a true lack of affection approaches these flowers, they leave on their skin a mark like that of a kiss.

Some single men grow these plants secretly, despite the warnings given to them by elderly women telling them that they will never get married if they do so. Most of them don't care—who should wish for a wife when they already receive her kisses?

The plant needs no water, which makes it even more attractive to the single men, and even more suspicious to the elderly women. Those women know that the flowers' kisses take much more than what they give.

White Hands

The old woman's hands were covered in brown blemishes. She always told her numerous grandchildren that they appeared when age had forced her to forget another song.

On the day of her funeral, there appeared a troubadour who, when he held her hand, began to sing the most beautiful old songs. By the time he stopped singing, her hands had turned completely white.

THE LITTLE BOY was a child of the storm. Only his mother knew that he had been conceived during that forbidden moment, and that his real father was an outcast who traveled from town to town invoking storms with his dark magic.

Towns were obligated to offer hospitality to those responsible for bringing the rain, but the house chosen by the mage was to be avoided by the town's residents for the rest of the year. That night, she was alone, and the terror that the storm produced in her drove her to find warmth and comfort in that strange man who barely talked. She has not seen him since the boy was born.

She knew that when her son turned thirteen years old, the storm would take him back. But she did not know how. "The worst that could happen," she would say to console herself, "is that he turns into a wretched traveler like his father."

The day, the minute, that the boy turned thirteen, there raged a storm so terrible that the very foundation of her house shook. This was unheard of, as there was no one near to invoke the storm. The mother forbade her son from leaving the house.

It was then that he said:

"If I don't leave, how will I receive my crown?"

His mother trembled. She had never told anyone.

"Today is the day in which I am to be named king," he said.

She went to embrace him, thinking that he must be feverish. She began to prepare him a bowl of wine soup while the thunder continued to roar.

A bolt of lightning tore through the roof of the house and struck the boy, transforming his head, for a long moment, into a crown of light.

Chapter 5: Trees

I

Ace of Trees

The Boy of Thorns shed all his spines except one, which marked the exact position of his heart.

The Boy of Thorns took the girl who had waited for him by the hand, and together they walked through the forest. They knew they could not kiss each other. They found an abandoned cabin, and they fixed it up so that they would have somewhere to live, to love. They spent four years together.

One day, a group of soldiers came knocking, and they took the girl. She was the daughter of a rich merchant, who had reported her missing many years ago.

The soldiers did, however, allow her to say goodbye to the boy. They could not help but kiss. As their lips parted, he fell to the floor. He was not asleep this time, no. He was dead, and the last of his thorns, the one that had remained next to his heart, withered and fell.

The girl picked up the thorn. When she returned to her father's house, she thought she would use it to make a spindle.

The Storm of Songs

Furious, the maestro threw a beautiful composition written by his student into the fire, saying that he was not ready to be writing his own melodies.

"Who do you think you are?"

Smoke poured from the chimney, extending over the town. Thunderous music echoed, loud enough for all to hear. The student knew exactly who he was.

“WHY DO YOU never want to play with that boy?

“He belongs to the cats,” she replied, the expression on her face rather distrustful as she continued licking her wrists.

THE POET TRACED the lines of his poem in dark ink, with only the soft glow of a candle to illuminate his words. Then, suddenly, one of his verses turned to gold. The poet, a bit apprehensive, read that verse once more. He didn’t consider it to be superior to any of the other verses he had written. He stopped writing and meditated for hours over that verse in particular, though he failed to come up with a satisfactory explanation and instead fell asleep.

The following morning, the poet went to investigate the curious golden verse, to see if it was still golden or if he had simply dreamt it. Much to his surprise, one verse was still traced in gold, but it was not the same one as the day before. The poet meditated over this new verse until the sun fell below the horizon. Once again, he fell asleep without understanding why that particular verse was different from any of the others.

That night, however, he had a dream: one of his hands had turned to gold, not the hand with which he wrote poems, but the hand he used to complete his daily chores, the hand he used to hold books, the hand he cupped to his ear when he struggled to hear.

When he woke, he knew what to do. He recited the two verses, one after the other, and realized that they only made sense together. He then wrote a third verse, a continuation of the two that came before. As he did, his hand, the one with which he wrote, began to glow softly, its light golden and warm.

II

Two of Trees

The Blue Flower

Every day, she would go to the garden to make sure that her lips were still redder than the red strawberries. She would visit the stables and would let out a sigh of relief when she saw that her skin was still whiter than the white milk. One day, however, in the meadow, she found a brilliant blue flower that was even bluer than her blue eyes. She plucked the flower from the ground so that nobody could ever compare them. Then, she went blind.

The traveler had to choose between three different trunks. He knew that the first held a priceless treasure, while the second held his certain death. And, in the third hid the key to solving a mystery, one that would open a path to true wisdom.

From one of the trunks came a ferocious growl, from another a nauseating odor, and the third shook violently, moving sporadically.

"What will happen if I choose none of the three trunks?" asked the traveler.

"In that case, one of the three will choose you, and it will follow you for as long as you live."

The traveler sighed, wondering how he could have possibly gotten into such a mess, and chose the growling trunk. He thought that with his sword, he could fend off any creature that had a throat.

"You have chosen well," they told him. "The white tiger costs a fortune."

"But it can also kill me."

"If you learn to tame it, though, you will be wiser for it."

How foolish, realized the traveler, to think that he ever really had a choice.

THE SEED OF Desire floats in the air. It is so small that it can be inhaled without its host even noticing.

Those who inhale the seed feel nothing strange for the first few weeks, but soon after, they are bothered by a tickle in their throat, one that encourages them to drink water from the river.

The Seed of Desire takes root, weaving its tendrils of aspirations and expectations through the flesh and blood of its host. It braids itself around nerves and brushes past entrails. It makes it impossible for the host to feel satisfied. Insatiable, the host will always need more, no matter the cost.

> THE SHOEMAKER WOKE one morning and saw that the job that he had not had time to finish the night before was now completely, perfectly finished, with stitching so fine that no human hand could have possibly done it. He brought the shoes as a gift to the Empress's daughter, and she was so delighted with the design that she asked to meet the creatures who made them.
>
> That night, the shoemaker was complaining at length about how poor he was and about how much it cost him to continue his work. When the sprites came to his aid, they got caught in the mousetraps that the shoemaker had set. The following day, he brought them to the daughter of the Empress.
>
> The girl took pity on the sprites and decided to release them from their traps so that they could live in a splendid dollhouse made by the imperial carpenter.
>
> The next day, the sprites were gone, and the Empress's daughter was found with her lips sewn shut. The stitches were so small that no human hand would ever be able to undo them.

III

Three of Trees

The fruit of the apple tree that grew in the cemetery was sacred. Only the spirits were entitled to them.

One day, unable to bear his gnawing hunger, an orphaned boy snuck over the wall and stole one of the apples that hung from the tree. He sank his teeth into its flesh, and from the fruit spilled blood.

Startled, he tried to flee the churchyard but found that he could not. An invisible force held him there. Truly desperate, he begged the spirits to let him go, and they replied that the apple could only be replaced by his own heart.

The boy accepted and left the cemetery. He felt an emptiness in his chest and his memory chill. He walked and walked, having very little idea of who he was, until he reached the village.

The sun shone in the morning sky, marking the start of a new day. Nobody seemed to realize what had happened to this orphaned boy. Why would they? They had all stolen an apple at one point in their lives, too.

The Badger's Ear

Around his neck, he wore the ear of a badger, which he had taken from the badger himself. Thanks to that amulet, he could hear the terrible swarms of bees as they approached, even from great distances. It was a power that awarded him fame and riches.

He unfortunately wore nothing that belonged to the bees. If he had, perhaps he would have heard the furious clan of badgers as they neared closer and closer.

THE AQUA FLOWER grew in his dreams. Sometimes, when withered ghosts haunted his memories and kept him from sleep, or when he jolted awake, choking on the unsettled dust of his past, he would leave his house and head to the river.

He would let the current wash over his hands. It was enough to calm him, to erase the thoughts that raced through his mind and replace them with images of the aqua flower. It was like a memory, instantaneous and vibrant, but he knew it was not, as he had never seen the aqua flower before.

He had, however, seen the people, now ghosts, who haunted his dreams. Their blurry images weighed on him and left his mouth dry every time he strayed from the river. The only permanent way to calm his suffering was to drown the ghosts until their dust turned to mud. The river welcomed his body, and his ghosts dissolved, turning forever into black sludge.

In his wake, the water created a beautiful, perfect, aqua flower for him to behold.

HER ENTIRE BODY was frozen, her skin an icy blue. It seemed as if she were dead, but a mirror placed below her nose proved that she still breathed. It was almost as if she were suffocating, but very slowly.

"Her wedding ring belongs to me," exclaimed the husband.

"We can't remove the ring without severing her finger. And a body that has been mutilated will not be well received by the gods."

"That is not my problem," he replied.

When they removed the ring, and her finger with it, the color returned to her body. She was lively again, and no longer married.

IV

FOUR OF TREES

THE QUEEN'S SCISSORS

AS THE QUEEN was giving birth, warriors invaded the palace. The queen ordered that her ring be tied to the navel of her child, hidden from sight. She then hid her newborn son among all the other infants.

Seven years later, the queen awaited seven candidates with a pair of sharpened scissors in her hand. There was only one way to know which was the true heir.

THE CHILDLESS WOMAN visited the same tree every afternoon, which was planted by her husband before he died. Some time had passed before she noticed that the trunk was beginning to swell, slowly growing wider over time. At one point, it seemed as if the tree were pregnant.

One morning, at dawn, the tree's belly tore open, giving birth to a little girl. The woman picked her up and gave her fresh water to drink. The girl's eyes were as blue as the eyes of the man she had once loved.

"I will only live for one day," cautioned the girl.

"Then I will do the same," replied the woman.

They spent that day by the river's edge and traveled to see the cascade of wild strawberries.

They passed beneath the Arch of Thoughts and laughed as they watched two young foxes play and fight.

At nightfall, they laid down in the grass, next to the tree. The tree bent down slowly and gently picked up their bodies. The woman who had never had children smiled and wondered why she had waited so long to do all those wonderful things.

THE OTHER PLAYERS were certain that the tallest one had cheated using the jack of clubs, though they had no proof.

The winner left the game, his pockets full and his face beaming with pride. His pride was soon extinguished by a sinking feeling that something bad was going to happen. Unbeknownst to him, someone waited outside. The attacker's eyes shone with a vengeful purpose. Never could the winner have guessed that his attacker would be dressed precisely as the jack of clubs.

V

Five of Trees

He Who Observes Teeth

When he was still quite young, he noticed that the teeth of herbivores and carnivores were different, and he began to assign people to one of the two categories. Most people, if they followed the diet he recommended, experienced a significant improvement in health.

He only lied one time. He lied to an avaricious and cruel leader, one who treated his town horribly.

He felt no remorse. He knew that the despot would not have listened to his advice anyway.

The doctor saw something shiny in the mouth of the fish he had just caught and recognized it immediately as a golden scale. It belonged to the King of the Fishes. These scales were not just scales but messages, which meant that the doctor had killed none other than the royal messenger as he was on his way to fetch the healer. He now had no choice but to help the king himself.

With a sigh of resignation, the doctor placed the scale in his mouth, waded into the water, and walked down to the bottom of the river.

Her mother explained to her that the storks were the ones who brought the babies, but even so, the little brother that she so desperately wanted still had not arrived. So, the girl waited until the stork had left its nest and then climbed to the top of the church's steeple to investigate. It was dangerous, but she knew that if she kept her eyes toward the sky, she could do it. When she reached the top, she searched inside the nest for her little brother, but all she could find was an egg. Maybe her brother was inside the egg, she thought.

With a great deal of caution, she placed the egg in her pocket and began to descend the tower. She was almost to the ground when the stork returned, furious. It pecked at her face, attacking her with its beak, eventually ripping out one of her eyes. An immense shock of pain flooded her body, but she still managed to reach the ground. She swatted the bird away and escaped to her house. Fortunately, the egg was still intact, and so she kept it safe and warm between the sheets of her bed. Only after did she tend to her wound.

The egg grew bigger and bigger, heavier and heavier, as the days passed.

When it finally hatched, there sat a smiling little boy. In his hands, he held a single, perfect eye.

SHE WENT TO visit the tomb of her grandson but could not find it. She attributed its supposed disappearance to her age, to her mental state, which was not what it once had been, and continued searching. Still unable to find it, even after confirming multiple times that she was in the right spot, she sat down on the bench, confused. If somebody had stolen the tombstone, then dirt would have been dug, and the grass would have been gone.

She closed her eyes for a moment and imagined that the death of her grandson had never come to pass. She opened her eyes again, hopeful, and glanced towards the spot where his tombstone once stood, where she had visited so many times before. The longer she stared at that miraculous spot, the more she managed to convince herself that her wish had come true, that she would return home to see her little boy standing there once again.

The boy's ghost, hopeful, knew that if his grandmother could convince herself beyond the shadow of a doubt that he was still alive, he would be able to return to her. He stayed as focused as he could, concentrating all his energy on maintaining his current form, green as the grass that grew from the earth.

VI

Six of Trees

ALL THE ADORNMENTS worn by the Empress, her earrings, bracelets, and necklaces, were small silver cages. Each one held a precious animal: a golden beetle, a firefly with a perennial glow, a blue fly, hummingbirds as small as an eyelash.

Every night, terrible ghosts haunted the Empress's dreams, ghosts of the spiders, salamanders, and mantises who died for her beauty. But she did not mind sleeping so little. Nothing makes a woman's features more beautiful. Nothing makes her seem more interesting and mysterious than having thick, dark circles sit under her eyes.

The Secret Tree

THE BLESSED LIQUOR distilled by the priest, which he made from the fruit of a secret tree, allowed those who drank it to forget their resentment. This liquor also burned the hands of sinners, though not the hands of the innocent. That is why the priest never touched his creation. And that is why he would never stop making it.

WHEN THE WOMAN visited the healer after her husband had beaten her, he did not heal her wounds but rather tattooed on her skin the image of a squid. None of the women understood what the tattoo meant. The next time her husband raised his hand in her direction, however, from the tattoo shot a thick cloud of ink that blinded him completely.

THE WHITE MOTH searches for its victims, who are also its home and its destiny. The white moth stalks them while they are awake and while they are asleep, desperate to press its lips against theirs and invade their dreams.

The black moth should never be killed. It is the only creature capable of stopping the white moth from piercing the lips of its victims and causing them an eternal ache of impossible desires.

VII

Seven of Trees

The People of the Stinging Nettle

The artisan spent several days sculpting. It was his most difficult piece yet, as he had to construct a hand for a girl who had lost her own to the people of the Stinging Nettle.

The hand that he created was so beautiful, he put so much care and effort into it, that the girl covered it with kisses.

The following day, she severed the hand that remained.

The people of the Stinging Nettle laughed that laugh of theirs, so reminiscent of the wind.

The least attractive girl in the village went to the fountain to fetch water just as she did every morning at the break of dawn. And, like every other day, she prayed along the way that her curse would finally end. Most people were ignorant of what hellish reality truly haunted her: instead of showing her true image, the water reflected back to her the face of an incredibly beautiful girl. Only the reflection's eyes were her own. She could not help but sit and admire this girl for a while. To contemplate an image so different from her own caused her as much happiness as it did misery.

It was then that a monstrous face appeared on the fountain's surface. The ugliest girl in the village jumped back, startled, bringing her hand to her chest. She spun around only to see that the reflection belonged to the neighboring town's most handsome man.

THE WINNER OF the poet's contest received, as a gift, one wound for every habitant that there was in the town. Each wound was different, and each left a different mark.

Nobody quite understood why that was considered a prize, and many poets refused to even enter the contest. But the winners wore their lesions and scars with pride, and they felt certain that the experience had made them better poets.

"So, suffering is your muse?" someone would inevitably ask.

"You could never understand," the poet would reply.

Each wound was completely different from the rest.

VIII

Eight of Trees

The Junivy Seed

"If you swallow a junivy seed, a vine will crawl from out of your mouth while you sleep and cover your face with a marvelously beautiful mask, though it will only last for one day. Once the ivy withers, however, your face will stay deformed and unrecognizable forever."

She never quite believed in that old wives' tale. But when they married her off to her father's most revolting, repugnant friend, she carried with her one of those seeds, hoping to slip it into his foul mouth. Just in case. And, just in case, she decided to believe in that old tale with all her might.

There is a man responsible for scaring children, and parents believe that to do so, he dyes his skin blue using moraga extract, turns his hair orange submerging it in brewed roots, and paints his teeth black with charcoal. Parents will pay him to yell at their children using a certain voice, feigned yet terrifying, shouting that they need to finish their beans, be obedient, that they shouldn't listen to other people's conversations through closed doors.

Sometimes, the scarer says a phrase that nobody has paid him to say to a girl who looks at him with wide eyes, held captive by her own fascination. Nobody notices what's happening. Several years later, that girl gives birth to a baby, one with blue skin, orange hair, and black teeth.

THE HAIRLESS WOMAN avoids men as she passes them on the street. She makes herself smaller so that she occupies as little space as possible. She hides from the light, and she keeps her eyes fixed on the ground, ashamed, as if she hoped that the earth would swallow her whole.

Occasionally, a man looks at her with a certain curiosity and observes her out of the corner of his eye, trying to imagine how that perfect body would look standing tall and positioned evocatively. When he catches a glimpse of her face, imagining it framed by a head of thick, golden curls and looks past her timidness and fear, he considers her quite beautiful.

Rarely does one of these onlookers approach her to make conversation. With patience, he manages to calm her, and, after several days, he even gets her to smile. When she finally warms up to her suitor, enough that she allows him to kiss her, he gathers the courage to ask:

"How did you lose it?"

She stares blankly, confused.

"Lose what?" she replies.

SHE HAD HEARD rumors about the magical qualities of shirts made from stinging nettle, and, since she had no greater desire than to escape her home, she gathered as many of those plants as she could and sewed them together in the shape of a shirt, thinking she might become a swan and fly far, far away.

She returned home, her hands and torso covered in terrible cuts, refusing to speak a word. Her mother beat her, like she always did, but the girl kept her lips shut. Furious and poisoned by bouts of liquor and misery, the girl's mother dragged her to the lake and held her head below its freezing waters.

It was then that the girl transformed into a swan.

IX

Nine of Trees

The Leafed Woman

He believed that the leafed woman was a figment of his imagination, only appearing in his dreams, yet he continued to write her verses and poems about birds and harps, and he left them near the apple tree.

The following summer, some of the apples had wings, while others had tiny chords.

As she finished peeling the last potato, about to add it to the ginormous pile, the most miserable of the royal kitchen maids found a ring that belonged to the king of the elves encapsulated by the vegetable. She knew that if she were to put on the ring, she would immediately become queen. Before she could decide for herself, the royal chef chopped off her fingers in a single hack, stealing the ring from the maid so that she could wear it herself. The moment she did, the king appeared suddenly, smiling.

He didn't even glance at the chef, who held her hand out, the ring shining, to claim her role as queen. Instead, he grabbed one of the potato peels and transformed it into a ring. He approached the peeler of tubers, took her mutilated hand, and slid the potato ring over where her finger would have been. The ring floated in the air and seemed as if it were made of pure gold.

The tiny red shoes were so beautiful, so brilliant, that the girl was certain they were charmed. She refused to try them on without first having done some sort of test. So, she made her grandparents' goose wear them.

The goose began to dance in the most ridiculous way, and the girl burst out laughing. She laughed and laughed as she watched its silly movements, a look of bewilderment drawn across its face.

Unable to control her laughter, she took pity on the goose and tried to remove the shoes from its feet. But she could not. Her attempt alone, however, was enough to get the goose to stop dancing, and it returned to its natural, calm state.

The girl, however, could not stop cackling. Her laugh was starting to suffocate her. Somehow, she found that even funnier.

THE SONG THAT he wished to sing was forbidden, but his desire to sing it grew stronger with the passing of each new day. The troubadour went to the witch in search of a solution.

"Would you prefer that I rid you of your desire to sing or that I make you forget that song? Be wary, however. If I rid you of your desire to sing, you will never be able to enjoy the performance of any other melody. If I force you to forget that forbidden song, you will never be able to learn it."

He chose to lose his desire to sing, despite how much he enjoyed singing. He took into consideration the fact that very few people knew the forbidden tune, and if he were to forget it, then it might disappear. The message that the forbidden song held was more important to him than his happiness.

When the troubadour found others like him and saw them enjoy their trade with joy and merriment, he accepted that they had simply made a different choice than he had. He envied their happiness, but he also knew that his life was more valuable than theirs.

X

Boy of Trees

There was a shawl that calmed the anxious. Simply placing it around a person's shoulders was enough to make all their worries disappear, or at least the ones that lived in their shoulders and back.

Mind you, nothing could erase the tiny blue tracks that their worries left behind as they fled.

The Boy Who Heard the Roots

When his granddaughter disappeared, the old king drew a mysterious map, and then he relinquished his soul. Even the wisest sages did not, could not, understand those capricious drawings.

It was then that the queen heard talk of a prodigious child. She covered the boy's eyes so that he would listen to the map without having seen it.

The boy began to walk, followed closely by the royal guards; he crossed rivers and climbed mountains, all to arrive at the nest of an eagle in which the remains of the little girl were found.

He could not figure out why the thistles, despite being an herb like any other, would emit heat. So, he asked his grandfather, who replied: "It is the heat of the battle. The little elves use their branches as swords. And the only thing that alleviates the pain of their battle wounds are the purple flowers that come from the branches of the thistle."

The boy knew that his grandfather spoke the truth because he had been a soldier for many years, and the boy also knew of the scars that covered his grandfather's body. Whenever it would storm, his grandfather would rub his aching knees and grip his left shoulder.

The next time it rained, the boy went to the forest to collect some of those purple flowers, not minding much that he could end up pricking his fingers in the process.

He was then ambushed and surrounded by an enormous army of tiny beings. He realized that they were there to protect the thistles. The boy tried to explain himself, but those ferocious green creatures did not understand his language. They knocked him to the ground and tied him up with rope made of grass and herbs. As they dragged him toward the magic circle, the boy's grandfather appeared from out of the woods, wielding his sword as the storm raged on.

The princess wished to obtain the golden line on the horizon so that she could fashion herself a bow. She asked each of her suitors to go find the line, but, out of them all, only one returned. This suitor brought her the horizon but warned her that if she were to adorn herself with it, she would become just as unattainable and lonely. The princess, however, did not understand what it was to be lonely, as she was always surrounded by servants and suitors. She looked at him and scoffed, placing the bow in her hair. She then told him to approach her, but he could no longer see her. She was as far away as the horizon.

XI

Maid of Trees

The Fountain of Time

"Why today?" asked the girl as she stood next to the stone fountain, waiting.

Whatever it was that approached her did not respond. It took five more steps.

"Give me just a bit more time," begged the girl.

"That is what I've spent all your life doing," replied the hooded figure, revealing a silver blade underneath its robe.

The girl glanced at her reflection in the water of the fountain. An old woman stared back.

In the depth and brilliance of the eyes, in their sundry colors, everything is written. Even so, the soothsayer always gives a choice to those who are bold enough to ask.

"I can either tell you how much time you have left in this life, or I can tell you your life's purpose."

Each person's choice eloquently expresses their fears, and the soothsayer knows that her response will only be able to calm one of them: the one whose answer remains a mystery.

The recently married man hung his ring from the branch of an elm tree so that he would not lose it as he bathed in the lake. But when he returned, he did not find the ring where he had left it.

Since trees suffer from the inability to move and it was impossible that his tree had fled, the newlywed believed that he had simply mistaken his tree for another. He inspected the other tree trunks and their branches, unsuccessful in his quest to find the ring. He looked to the skies, thinking it might have been a magpie who took it, but he saw not a single one.

It was then that an incredibly beautiful young woman appeared, and she was wearing his ring. She was dressed in a tabard whose color was identical to the color of the leaves that hung from the elm.

The newlywed realized his mistake, that the woman was the tree he was searching for, and that he had unintentionally wed her. So, he drew his sword and chopped down her trunk.

The rest of the tree let their leaves fall to the ground, mourning her death.

THE KING HAD ordered all the trees whose trunks were hollow to be cut down, since everyone knew that those hollowed trunks were the wombs from which witches were born. He mobilized his army so that they could complete the operation in a single night. That very night, the queen fell ill.

The only cure for the queen's fatal illness was a flower that only the witches recognized. There remained very few witches, however, and they all hated the king.

"Father, I am also a witch," said the princess, her eyes full of tears. "My nanny taught me their forbidden secrets. I will go to the forest, and I will save Mother."

What a shame that the king had sworn to kill all witches.

XII

Jack of Trees

The Firefly

The girl believed that fireflies were the most beautiful creatures in all the world, and she asked one to marry her. The insect blinked three times. The girl grew older and ended up forgetting about what had occurred.

Years later, she gave birth to a child who never opened his eyes. He was gentle and had a good heart, and his mother loved him as much as she did herself.

One night, looking in from outside the window, something blinked three times. Her memories came flooding back, and she was frightened of what those three blinks meant. She ran to her son's room. Frightened, the child opened his eyes, and from them shone a light so bright that his mother was blinded forever.

> There was a country in which it was said that giving birth to two children at once was a blessing from the gods. When twins were born, the residents of each town would do their utmost, providing the family with innumerable gifts.
>
> Twelve years later, they took their children.

The queen ordered that her maids prepare her a bath of puppy blood every day. But her maids would trick her, giving her instead a bath made of beet juice and salty wine.

The queen asked them to keep the puppies' skin, with the intention of making a coat. But her maids found a moss so smooth that, once dry and oxidized, could trick the queen.

But when the queen asked for the puppies' bones to build herself a throne, the maids had nothing to give her. The queen discovered their tricks and ordered their execution. That night, a furious pack of wild hounds destroyed the doors to the palace and devoured the queen.

HER GLOVES COVERED the slender silhouette of her long, feminine fingers.

The gloves also kept the sharp crow beaks closed that she had in place of nails.

XIII

Sage of Trees

"What is the cause of your sadness?" asked the chanting monks. But the boy, whom the monks had raised, could not speak. He would have told them that he was going to miss them. He liked to listen to their chants, the ones that honored the angels.

That night, in complete silence, the boy disappeared into the sky. After that moment, the rain tasted just the slightest bit salty. The monks knew that the angels, though they do not sing, carry music within.

The Key that Sprouts from the Tree

After years and years of study and persistent pursuit, he learned in which forest the key would sprout, and there he went. But the key had sprouted at the top of the tallest tree, and he could not reach it, nor could he speak the same language as the birds. Defeated, he rested against the trunk of the tree. It was then that he heard the ants speak.

The woman knew that she had a knot in her heart because she felt pain that was shaped just like one. She thought that only the fingers of a ghost, able to pass through her flesh without damaging it, could undo the knot. She searched abandoned watchtowers, battlegrounds, and haunted castles. She was startled so many times that her hair turned completely white, but not a single ghost stopped to listen to her.

Then, she saw her. A ghost was standing next to an alabaster window as translucent as she was, and her heart was knotted. She reached into the ghost's chest and, though it was complicated, undid the knot. The ghost smiled for a moment, and then dissipated into the air. But her smile was so kind, so sincere, that it was enough to dissolve the woman's own pain.

"CHOOSE WHERE YOU prefer that I hurt you," said the swordsman.

"We shall both follow the course of the river," said his rival, panting.

"As you wish," was his reply.

The swordsman severed the main artery of his defeated rival and guided the trickling blood toward the river with his sword.

The moment his blade touched the water, the winner was shown his true reflection.

IT WAS ONLY possible to see wings of sorrow in a mirror polished with tears. These wings were unique to each person, but the nuns never told visitors if their wings were stronger or weaker than others'. They simply gave medicine to the weakest.

The mother superior, responsible for all remedies, doubted greatly their efficacy. Her face was sullen, and her eyes exhausted. Soon, nothing would remain of her body except her wings.

XIV

Elder of Trees

Devil's Track

Her grandmother taught her to always keep a bit of salt in her pockets. Every time she saw mushrooms called "devil's track," she was to sprinkle salt over them. This would keep the devil from traveling the world. But the girl was no longer a girl, and salt was quite expensive, and she had long since stopped believing in such wives' tales. One day, she saw the mushrooms but decided to keep the salt instead to give to her lover as a gift. She simply stomped on the mushrooms and continued on her way.

The mushrooms, now ripped from the ground, followed slowly behind.

> It is said that the most beautiful of the nymphs, when she is not naked, wears a dress made of the eyelids of all those who spied on her while she bathed.

The baby was born with all his teeth. The queen was frightened of her own son and avoided looking at him whenever possible. The maids whispered behind her back, calling her a horrid mother, among other worse things. The baby cried and cried. He missed his mother. His teeth grew sharper with the passing of each day, and the maids said that it was because of the pain he felt.

The queen asked the mother of her husband if he had also been born that way, and she replied that he had not.

Then, she went to visit her own mother, who lived quite far from the palace, and asked her the same question. Her mother spoke not, but rather lifted her blouse to reveal destroyed breasts.

"Why did you breastfeed me? Why did you never tell me?"

"Because you are my daughter, and because you are my daughter."

The queen returned to the palace and offered her son her perfect breasts.

"If I had known, I would not have died," replied the ghost.

He who had been his lover began to cry like he had never cried before.

Acknowledgments

I would like to thank Lawrence Shimel for his invaluable help with this book, as he translated many of these stories so that they could be published in English, Santiago Eximeno, Lluís Salvador, and Jaime Gabaldà. Also, Francesc Miralles, who put me in touch with the siren Nuria González Carretero, and through her I discovered the otherworldly art of Anna Ribot.

This book would not have been able to exist if I had not read the short stories of my admired Anna María Shua and Espido Freire.

English versions of some of these stories, all of them translated by Lawrence Schimel, appear in the following:

EL JABATO, "The Magic Walnut" (nominated for The Rhysling and Dwarf Stars Awards), *Mythic Delirium*, 25, Summer/Fall 2011; 2012 Rhysling Anthology.

LA VENTANA MÁGICA, "The Magic Window," *Mythic Delirium*, Issue 27, Summer/Fall 2012.

EL SUEÑO DEL TABERNERO, "The Inkeeper's Dream," *Space and Time*, #116, Spring 2012.

EL ANILLO DORADO, "The Golden Ring," *Star Line*, October-December 2011.

LA DORADA LÍNEA DEL HORIZONTE, "The Golden Line of the Horizon," *Strange Horizons*, August 6, 2012.

LA LUCIÉRNAGA, "The Firefly," *Dreams & Nightmares*, #96, 2013.

SOFÍA RHEI

Madrid, 1978. She is a writer, with more than fifty publications. Her work has been translated into various languages. She frequents festivals and conventions for literature of the fantasy genre.

She has published poetry books: *Las flores de alcohol* (La bella Varsovia, 2005), *Química* (El gaviero, 2000), *Otra explicación para el temblor de las hojas* (Premio Zaidín de Poesía Javier Egea. Ayuntamiento de Granada, 2007), *Alicia Volátil* (Cangrejo Pistolero, 2010), *Bestiario microscópico* (Sportula, 2012), *La simiente de la luz* (Lapsus Calami, 2014) y *La belleza de la bestia* (Lapsus Calami, 2015), and the children's poetry book, *Adivinanzas con beso para las buenas noches* (Alfaguara, 2014).

Her narrative works include the young reader's fantasy novels *Flores de sombra* (Alfaguara, 2011) and its sequel *Savia Negra*; numerous children's books, including *El picaro Nasrudin* (Loquelo, 2016), *Cuentos y leyendas de objetos mágicos* (Anaya, 2001), *La Calle Andersen* (coauthored by Marian Womach. La Galera, 2014), *Olivia Shakespeare* (Edelvives, 2014), and *Cómo tener ideas* (Narval, 2016); the children's series *Krippys* (Montena), *El joven Moriarty* (translated in various languages, mentioned by Banco del Libro de Venezuela. Fábulas de Albión, 2013-2015), *Los hermanos Mozart* (Disquesí Ediciones, 2015).

She was awarded the Spirit of Dedication prize in 2016 by the European Science Fiction Society for her work in children's literature.

In 2019, she published the short fiction collection *Everything is Made of Letters* (Aqueduct Press).

Her adult novels include *Róndola*. She was awarded the Premio Celcius in 2017 in the category of Best Science Fiction and Fantasy Novel (Minotauro, 2016) and *Espérame en la última página* (Plaza y Janés, 2017).

ANNA RIBOT URBITA

Graduated from the Escola Massana, Arts and Design school in Barcelona with a degree in Pictorial Techniques. She has held expositions in numerous cities throughout Spain and Europe, and has received distinguished institutional awards. Her illustrations have appeared in the books *El flabiol dels flabiolaires* and *Introducció al flabiol i bombo*, both with Editorial Altafulla, 2001; *Calendari de Mitologia 2016* and *Calendari de Mitologia 2017*, both with Editorial Montnegre; *Viatge del torderenc Pere Porter a les calderes de Pedro Botero*, Círculo de Historia-Ayuntamiento de Tordera, 2017.

KENDAL SIMMONS

A translator and editor from New York. Her previous translations include Vassar College's *The Oviedo Project*.